The Magic Bullet

Bill Keith

"Books for the Journey"

StoneGate Publishing Company

Longview 2010

StoneGate Publishing Co., Inc.
P. O. Box 8321
Longview, TX 75607
StonegateBooks@aol.com

The jagged New Orleans skyline was barely visible through the early morning mist washing the city as V. J. Casstevens hurried through the fabled French Quarter to his office on Chartres Street. The events of the past few days flashed through his mind like a bad movie – the ominous phone call from the director's secretary and the toilet gossip that he would be fired.

And everyone knows I've reached a dead end in my research.

But he had no way of knowing that he was about to be caught up in a web of treachery and intrigue and would become a suspect in the worst crime in the history of the City of New Orleans.

A cool breeze from the prevailing winds of the Gulf of Mexico felt good on his face but he could not enjoy it for he had a sinking feeling in the pit of his stomach and feared the uncertain future.

V. J. stopped at the Market Café for *beignets* and cappuccino to try to settle his nerves and watched the pigeons scurry across the floor picking up crumbs. He drank the cappuccino, ate the *beignets* and licked the powdered sugar from his fingers then left the cafe and walked up the stairs to the promenade on the River Walk where he glanced back at the Quarter.

He had experienced his own private love affair with the Quarter during his ten years of research at the National Science Research Center. It was a hideaway where he could live out his illustrated adult fable and find relief from the battering life gives a man. He often felt seduced by the Quarter and its music – the rockish shards and jazz riffs – and by the bravura of clashing cultures, Cajun, Creole and the others.

I love it and will miss it if I lose my job.

The Center was housed in a grand old red brick building that once was a brewery. It was a hundred years old and built as they once built them but don't build them anymore.

V. J. pushed open the ornate wood doors made of polished Cypress with beautiful hand carvings by Cajun artisans of an earlier generation. He waved at the Pinkerton security guard in the foyer then stepped inside the elevator, pulled the hand lever and waited impatiently as the archaic lift squeaked its way to the fifth floor.

When the elevator door opened, he met Roscoe Chan, director of public relations at the Center.

"Eh, Ponce de Leon, still looking for the genie in the bottle?" Chan asked with a sheepish grin on his sallow face. V. J. ignored him. Chan was one of a dozen or more who had made fun of him and his research since the day he arrived.

He walked down the hall toward the director's office and met two lab assistants who made like monkeys, scratching under their armpits and jumping up and down.

"Gonna be a rough day, eh Doctor?" one of them said.

"I guess they all know I'm in trouble with the director," he said under his breath as he approached the office.

Weegie Peabody, the director's secretary, looked up

over her reading glasses dangling far down on her pointed nose and said, with an air of indifference, "Dr. Casstevens, the director will see you in a few minutes." Then she began tugging at her skirt as though embarrassed that he could see her knotty knees.

He rubbed his three-day growth of whiskers. "Yeah, Weegie."

She was a middle-aged, hard-bodied blond and V. J. thought she had worn well during half a century. *But she has had so many facelifts and her face is so tight, I bet every time she sits down her mouth pops open. And she really needs to do her roots. Boy, do I have an attitude today, or what? But she does have the prettiest green eyes.*

"Weegie, I'm going down to the men's room to get a little relief, if you know what I mean, and wash up. Be right back."

She arched her left eyebrow.

V. J. inserted his key into the lock on the toilet door, stepped inside and over to a urinal where he read the crude graffiti scratched on the wall. One of the inscriptions said: "Please stand up close – the guy next in line may be barefooted." He chuckled, and read another that said: "Don't throw your butts in the toilet, they're hard to light when they get wet." He always liked to read the graffiti for he had written most of it.

After taking care of business at the urinal, he went to the lavatory to wash his hands and face. He looked in the mirror and saw his red bloodshot eyes where blue eyes used to be, and his chiseled jaw almost hidden by his beard. The picture in the mirror made him feel like an old man in a young man's body. He winced when he saw his stomach hanging over his Abita Amber Beer belt buckle.

"Look what the good life in the French Quarter has

done for you, Casstevens."

He returned to the director's office, glanced through the open door and saw Dr. Strobe McPheeters, a man he called "The Executioner," talking to the director. After the scientists at the Center removed the animals' livers or kidneys, transplanted dogs' hearts into pigs and pigs' bellies into chimpanzees, if the animals rejected the transplants, McPheeters killed them by lethal injection. V. J. didn't like him.

Sitting there looking at Weegie Peabody still trying to cover her knees, he wondered why she didn't wear a longer skirt.

As he tried to eavesdrop on the director's conversation with "The Executioner," his emotions ran the gamut somewhere between regret and deliverance as he reflected on his ten years of research working with chimpanzees trying to find the magic bullet that would solve the mystery of aging.

It was only a stupid dream ten years ago and it's only a stupid dream today. It will never happen. People get old and die and there's nothing that can be done about it. And there's really nothing new under the sun – whatever was will be again. And this center is an intellectual wasteland of scientific theory where the perceptive get bored with long committee meetings, circular arguments about the trivial, the abstract and the incomprehensible.

He knew his career in aging research really was little more than a game bordering on a scam. *But the game may be over.*

"It all began at a fraternity party when I was in graduate school in Cal Tech," he once told Macee Marineaux, a friend he liked to hang out with in the Quarter at night. "Several of the fraternity brothers got tanked up on beer and started talking about how to run a scam on the government and get some grant money, which is what science is all about."

That night he decided to call his grant request the "Fountain of Youth Project" and suggest to the National Institutes for Health in Bethesda, Maryland, that with proper funding he might be able to find the key that would unlock the door to life extension.

"After I sobered up the next day, I filled out all the necessary papers, attached reams of questionable scientific studies on aging from Europe and the Middle East, and mailed them to Bethesda," he told her. "Three months later I received a reply that the project was being funded and I was to report here to New Orleans after I received my Ph.D. in microbiology."

That was the beginning of his incarnation as a government scientist.

Dr. Peter Mark Townsend, the director of the Center, immediately showed his contempt for V. J.'s project. He assigned him an office next to the animal cages in the basement where they kept the chimpan-zees, dogs, rats and rabbits and a host of other lab ani-mals, including a few pigs.

"Townsend could have found me a real office instead of putting me down there with the animals," he said, "but maybe it was a blessing in disguise." He loved the animals and thought they were better adjusted to their confinement than some of the scientists were to their freedom.

V. J. often waited until the other scientists went home at night to use the cancer and AIDS research labs on the second and third floors. He grinned when he remembered the night he turned all the chimpanzees loose in the cancer lab. He was alone in the Center, except for the Pinkerton guard, and thought it would be

fun to see a little action in the drop-dead serious atmos-
phere of the Center and give the chimps some relief
from the monotony of confinement to their cages.

"Macee, it looked like a jailbreak. The chimps ran
wild through the building swinging from light fixtures,
running the old elevator up and down the shaft,
smoking cigars pilfered from the director's office and
pecking at typewriters."

That night Rufus, the oldest chimp at the Center
who was four feet tall and weighed about ninety
pounds, went into the director's office and sat down at
the desk to smoke a cigar, one of the several bad habits
V. J. had taught him.

"That's a real monkey house in there, isn't it Rufus?"
The chimp smiled through a hint of breathy laughter,
gave a couple of pant-hoots, clapped his hands and continued puffing on the cigar.

V. J. always had a fundamental irreverence for au-
thority and as he watched his old friend Rufus and the
other chimps having such a good time, he realized they
were free of all emotional pollution. He laughed out
loud when he saw Rufus answer the call of nature right
on top of the director's new desk.

"Rufus, no! Stop that!"

The chimp stood up straight, flashed his butt to V. J.
and walked around to the front of the desk and kissed
him on the cheek.

V. J. laughed, wiped the chimp's slobber from his
face with his shirtsleeve and killed the last half of a can
of beer with one swig. Then he crushed the can with his
hand and threw it across the room into a wastebasket.

The Pinkerton guard was half-asleep in the foyer
and knew nothing of the ruckus the chimps were making inside the lab until one of them accidentally tripped

the fire alarm. A few minutes later a half-dozen fire trucks, sirens screaming and lights flashing in the foggy New Orleans night, pulled up in front of the Center. The guard saw the fire trucks and wouldn't have been more surprised if someone had launched him from Cape Canaveral.

V. J. heard the sirens, grabbed Rufus by the hand and led him to a secret passage that ran from the Center through an abandoned building next door and down toward the river.

Townsend, who had picked up the fire alarm on his police scanner, helped the firemen round up the chimps and return them to their cages.

"Now all the fun is over, old buddy," V. J. told Rufus as they sat in the dark passageway drinking Abita Amber Beer, brewed in Abita Springs across Lake Ponchartrain from New Orleans.

V. J. also explained to Macee how he found the secret passage, quite by accident. "There was an old wine cellar in a dark corner of the first floor with dozens of broken bottles in an ornate wood wine cabinet. One day I felt a cool breeze blowing through a hole in the cabinet and, curious, moved it away from the wall. I brushed away the cobwebs, struck a match and found a passage through which I could see a shaft of light in the distance."

The next day he brought a flashlight from home and he and Rufus explored the passage. "It was cool and damp and extended nearly a hundred yards down toward the river," he said. "When I reached the end, I found a steel grate, covered with dirt and debris. I brushed away the trash then pushed up on the grate, surrounded by a heavy growth of vines and bushes, and it opened. I crawled out and could see the river in the distance."

V. J. often felt smothered in arrogance by the other scientists at the Center. So, when he could no longer endure, he took Rufus to the hiding place to relax and drink the beer he kept in an ice chest there. It was a fantasy world away from the real world where he could hide and think and dream. And he enjoyed sitting in the dark but sometimes both he and the chimp drank too much, passed out and slept the night there.

"You can always remember things in the dark – things you're afraid to face in the daylight," he told Rufus one night.

V. J. waited impatiently for the firemen to leave. He put his arm around Rufus and realized how much they were alike – they both smelled of chloroform, were drinking buddies and best friends.

The director went to his office and saw the chimp's big brown dingle berry right in the middle of his desk, all coiled up like a snake about to strike. He turned red with anger, threw a paperweight and broke a mirror on the wall and stomped out of the building.

The next morning the *New Orleans Times-American* newspaper reported the chimps did a half-million dollars in damage to research projects in progress. V. J. thought the report was grossly exaggerated. "There was some damage, but it was fun and a temporary relief from the monotony of his search for the magic bullet that would solve the mystery of aging," he told Macee.

Everyone, including the director, knew that V. J. had turned the chimps loose. But no one could prove it and he certainly would never admit it.

Weegie Peabody, with a voice soft and small, interrupted his journey into the past. "Dr. Casstevens, the director will see you now."

"Thanks, Weegie."

V. J. wiped sweat from his forehead with his shirtsleeve and tried to stop his hands from shaking. He knew the director was not well glued together and no one at the Center could ever guess what he was going to do.

This could turn out to be one of those days I can't scrape off so easily.

"Come in Casstevens."

V. J. looked down at the diminutive director. *This guy fascinates me and even irritates me a little. But one thing is for sure, he's always good for a laugh or two, especially when he gets excited and his dentures start to click and he whistles and even hisses a little when he talks. Boy, would I like to set off a firecracker under his butt to see how far his false teeth would fly.*

A wide grin creased V. J.'s bearded face.

"Something funny, Casstevens?"

"No, not really."

The director fumbled through a set of papers. "So, Victor Jefferson Casstevens, undergraduate degree from Stanford and Ph. D. from the California Institute for Technology, working here at the Center for ten years."

The director's mustache stiffened and his words sounded pre-recorded. He shifted around in his chair like he had just been goosed by a poltergeist or had a bad case of hemorrhoids.

"Casstevens, you've been here quite a long time and, as far as I can tell, you've produced nothing."

V. J. grinned. "Yeah, that's about it." He knew he had been doing very little but he had been doing it well and some goals are so worthy its glorious even to fail.

"Everyone here at the Center knows you've been running a scam on the government all these years and making seventy five grand a year while doing it. You've searched for the Holy Grail and returned empty-handed. No critical research, no scientific papers and no magic bullet."

V. J. tried to disguise his fear. "But my time hasn't been wasted. I've developed a keen interest in cross-word clues, cryptic messages and New Orleans ghosts."

"Don't get smart with me, Casstevens!"

V. J. grinned. "I've run some tests."

"What have you found?"

He did not reply.

"Well, do you have anything serious to say on your behalf?"

"Look, Townsend, I don't want to guess, I don't want to tap dance, I don't want to play games – just give it to me straight."

"Okay, I'm terminating your contract with NIH effective the first of next month. Your sins have returned to visit you and you will no longer be selling your snake oil around here."

"You know, Townsend, this place is a circus – you terminate me and continue the cancer and AIDS research and your doctors, with all their scholarly papers being published in prestigious journals have found nothing, zero that will help a cancer or AIDS person live one day longer."

The director glared at him so hard V. J. thought he was going to pop a vein on his forehead.

V. J.'s his left eye began to twitch, a sign he was getting mad. "Maybe something good can come from this. I'll no longer be forced to endure the elitist arrogance from you and all your egocentric scientists."

Townsend's nerves seemed to be sucking the life out of his battery as he continued shifting around in his chair.

"Sometimes the weirdest things in life are true and the truest things are weird. Yeah, my research has led to a dead end but my time was not all wasted. I've conducted hundreds of tests on the chimps and, although the results were inconclusive, I believe there really may be a magic bullet that will prolong life, perhaps for many years."

"You know that's a fool's theory."

"Maybe I'm just a fool. Well, I guess that just about does it, don't it? How do I get out of this mausoleum?"

V. J. felt like he was holding on to a bad-luck charm.

"I'll expect you out of your office by the end of the week," the director said as though pronouncing the final sentence of his excommunication. "And if I were you I would –"

"If you were me, I would be embarrassed."

The director's mouth dropped open and he had a shocked look on his face.

V. J. walked out of the office with neither a farewell nor apology. He winked, puckered his lips and blew Weegie Peabody a kiss then disappeared down the hall.

He sat down at his desk in the basement and reflected on getting fired and wondered what it would be like trying to find a new job and working for wages.

Probably pure hell.

CHAPTER TWO

V. J. reached across his cluttered desk and picked up a little yellow rubber duck and squeezed it a couple of times and glanced at a picture of the Green Hornet, his favorite comic book character, taped to the side of a file cabinet.

I guess I have learned a few things these past ten years but all I know for sure is that hope is long and memory short and research into the causes and cure for aging is full of shooting stars that often crash and burn.

Through the years he believed there might be a magic bullet that would target and neutralize the disease that causes aging and even reverse the process. Is there a biological clock in each human being that defines the life span? He often wondered. But he doubted if he or any other scientist would ever find it.

V. J. often dreamed of an ageless world with youthful treasures that defy science and imagination. It would not be a Fountain of Youth *per se,* but the dream of ageless living fascinated him for it was so mysterious.

Anyway, one of the biggest problems with success is that its recipe is about the same as for a nervous breakdown – and I sure don't need that.

He often read the works of Professor Yakob Venter of the Israeli Aging Research Institute in Tel Aviv who discovered a body function called "senescence" where living cells grow old and stop dividing and begin to deteriorate. He and Professor Venter often corresponded and in one letter the professor said, "Conceptually and theoretically, the secret of human longevity – our future, our destiny – is the secret of the renewal of youth and I believe the time will come when scientists will find the answer to that secret."

V. J. wrote in his response to Professor Venter. "I know the human body is the most complicated presence in the world. Will that body, that presence, one day surrender its genetic clock and help us stay young for a long, long time?"

Dr. Venter replied. "That would be a miracle, a wonderful dream come true, and this old earth would become an Eden again in a spectacular genesis of a new world. I know the biochemical pathway in aging is quite complex but even the remote possibility of an elixir that would solve this biological problem is worth every effort of scientific inquiry."

V. J. also read and reread the works of Professor Paul Erlich of Germany who won the Nobel Peace prize in the area of physiology of medicine in 1908 and is well known for his research in hematology, immunology and chemotherapy. Erlich was the scientist who coined the term "magic bullet" which he defined as a magical cure for disease and his research was the subject of a major motion picture which V. J. had seen a dozen times.

V. J.'s independent study of cell biology revealed the existence of "telomeres" that he believed make up the major genetic time clock. He believed these were cell structures attached to the ends of chromosomes that protect the cells and assist in their reproduction. He also wondered about numerous enzymes that seem to have prolonged longevity. *Could they be the agents of a longer and healthier life? I know one thing for sure, I must find a growth catalyst that will allow cells to divide a thousand or ten thousand times rather than dying after only a few replications.*

Through the years he learned the origin of aging probably takes place before birth when a process, mysterious and unknown, interrupts the normal function of the genes that control aging, genes that also cause the migration and differentiation of cells.

Hundreds of unanswered questions intrigued him.

As he sat at his desk reliving the failures of the past ten years, he suddenly felt a strange premonition, like an omen. He knew he must conduct one last experiment.

That evening after the other scientists left the Center, V. J. went to the cancer lab on the second floor to conduct his final experiment and use an electron high-resolution microscope, which magnifies cells one million times, and the image splitter that sends images from the microscope into two cameras then to a computer monitor. One was an Optical Doppler Velocemeter that measures the movement of red blood cells. The second was a fluorescence detection camera. The computer collects and stores the data from the cells which are about one-one-thousandth of an inch in size then analyzes the data and prepares it for study.

"Okay, Casstevens, let's get it right this time. One more shot! Seven come eleven on a rusty dime and hang in there one more time."

He took a small vial of the blood he had removed from Rufus. He placed it in a centrifuge to separate the different substances by whirling the blood at high speeds as he prepared to study their chemical content and activity. He removed the blood from the centrifuge and returned it to a vial.

He looked at the cells through an electron micro-scope. "These little guys all have special jobs to do. They are almost like miniature chemical factories within themselves."

V. J. studied the blood sample then went to an in-cubator -- with a gaseous environment of thirty-sev-en-degrees centigrade -- and removed some other cells taken from a much younger chimp a few days earlier. He walked over to a Bunsen burner and sterilized his instruments before transferring the cells from flasks to several plates. Then he returned to the electron micro-scope to examine the two sets of cells.

"I'm looking for that elusive magic bullet," V. J. said as he examined the cells, tiny masses of protoplasm that form the basic unit of all living things. He knew the ex-periment would be number seven hundred sixty two and probably his last.

"Fate, destiny or even pure luck – I'll take anything, come on and speak to V. J."

Suddenly he realized he was sweating. He wiped the palms of his hands on his jeans then raised his arm and wiped his forehead with a paper towel.

"A human has ten trillion cells, wonder how many a chimp would have?"

He looked at the molecules in the cells and tried to identify them structurally for they all had different characteristics.

"One more experiment – the final dance for the mad scientist. What keeps these little guys from fatigue and death at the hands of those devil free radicals?"

During hundreds of experiments he worked with certain enzyme molecules, small guards or facilitators attached to large molecules like proteins. His chemistry professor at Stanford had explained to him that these enzymes are found in all living things and speed up certain chemical reactions in other cells.

His professor explained it this way: "They function by changing other molecules then blend with the changed molecules to form an intricate molecular structure which provides the environment in which chemical reactions can take place."

V. J. continued to study the enzyme molecules for nearly an hour. "I've watched you little rascals for years – you're the spark plugs that cause all kinds of chemical reactions, maybe as many as a million times a minute. But which one holds the mysterious secret of the elusive magic bullet that can trigger hundreds, even thousands of replication reactions?"

V. J. believed a certain enzyme or enzymes might inhibit the free radicals that cause the death of the cells. But all his experiments had produced no clue to support the theory.

"What about this one? Okay hoochie mama, a little *Lagniappe* for V. J. Casstevens. Maybe it's worth a shot."

He removed the enzyme from one of the cells taken from the younger chimp. Although he had seen the enzyme numerous times, he had never isolated it for research. He often referred to it as Enzyme-X and decided to include it in his experiment.

"Tonight is your night."

He removed the Enzyme-X molecule then transferred it to the sample of blood taken from Rufus. Suddenly the cells around the Enzyme-X molecules began to replicate right before his eyes.

"That's encouraging, no, it's rather astounding."

V. J. reasoned if he could isolate and remove that same enzyme molecule from enough cells, he might see a stronger reaction so he decided to remove dozens of the Enzyme-X molecules from the cells of the blood of the young chimp.

He began to sing somewhat off key and did a Cabbage Patch dance in front of the microscope. "It don't mean a thing if it ain't got no swing. Uh huh, uh huh, I'm doing it, I'm doing it!" he yelled, as he watched the cells repeat their replication process thousands of times. The more enzymes he removed and added to Rufus' blood, the greater the reaction as cells all around them spread to other cells causing them to replicate.

V. J. was so excited he had to go to the bathroom to keep from soiling his shorts. He washed his face and went to the break room where he brewed a pot of Community Coffee with Chicory and considered the chilling ramifications of his experiment. His brain was spinning so fast he pinched himself to make sure he wasn't in some mode of astral travel on his way to Mars or Jupiter or on his way home.

"Am I just dreaming? Could this Enzyme-X be the catalyst to alter the genetic code that governs aging?"

He drank four or five cups of the thick black chicory coffee and returned to the lab where he worked throughout the night removing the Enzyme-X molecules from hundreds of other cells from the blood of the younger chimp.

"Now, will it work on Rufus? Well, easy come, easy go. I'll give the old chimp a shot and fate can take it from there."

V. J. approached the chimp's cage holding a syringe in his left hand and a can of beer in his right. Rufus jumped up and down and snorted. V. J. opened the cage and the old chimp licked his face and rested his head on his shoulder then settled down and began drinking the beer. He injected him with the thousands of Enzyme-X molecules from the younger chimp's blood cells.

V. J. closed the screen door of the cage and locked it. "Like the old song says, 'Whatever will be, will be.' See you in a few days, old buddy."

V. J. was not aware that his experiment had been observed through a well-concealed video camera, one of three in the Center that monitored the Cancer and AIDS Research Labs and V. J.'s office in the basement.

A large man with a shaved head and handlebar mustache, wearing pince-nez glasses and a muscle shirt, sat before a video monitor in his room on the top floor of the Hotel St. Marie on Toulouse Street, a half block off Bourbon Street. He watched V. J.'s experiment with great interest and later carefully reviewed the video of the experiment. Then the big man picked up the phone and dialed Chicago.

"Culverwell Suite," Frankie D'Angelo, a ranking security officer for Culverwell Enterprises, said.

"This is Star Gazer in New Orleans. Let me speak to Mr. C."

"He's already retired for the evening."

"Then wake him up – we may have an alpha-positive."

"Okay." D'Angelo was aware that "alpha-positive" was the code name for a major discovery that would be of interest to Alexander Culverwell, the founder and president of Culverwell Enterprises in Chicago.

He rapped softly on the bedroom door. "Mr. C, it's Star Gazer."

Culverwell picked up the phone beside his bed. "This is C, talk to me, Star Gazer."

"Mr. C, I believe we have an alpha-positive."

"Based on what premise?"

"This Dr. Cassstevens at the Science Center was running an experiment on a vial of blood serum taken from one of the young chimpanzees and during the test he seems to have found a way for young cells to replicate and renew the old cells in an older chimp's blood."

"Yes, please continue."

"The doctor observed the experiment through a powerful microscope that transferred the pictures of the replication to a computer monitor. I saw it myself and have it on video."

"You may have something. Send me the video immediately by special courier plane and my scientists will examine the data and try to determine exactly what Dr. Cassstevens has discovered."

"Mr. C, I've observed this guy for years and I've never seen him get excited about anything related to his work until tonight. And if he has found something, I suggest you activate the recovery team and have them stand by for deployment to New Orleans to grab him and escort him back to Chicago without delay."

"Yes, Star Gazer, we'll call in the team tonight and tell them to stand by and wait until we determine if the research is credible."

"I'll monitor the situation here for a few more days and keep in touch with you."

"And I want to hear from you every few hours."

V. J. returned to his apartment at 4 a.m. but was so excited he couldn't sleep. His mind was flying at warp speed thinking about the experiment. He finally dozed off after daylight.

He woke up early in the afternoon and decided to take the day off and hang out in the Quarter with Macee in the evening. He knew it didn't matter if he went to work or stayed home since no one at the Center, except Rufus, would miss him.

The next day Culverwell informed Star Gazer that the scientists from the Culverwell Institute reviewed the video and were convinced that Dr. Casstevens may have made a very promising discovery.

Culverwell's aging voice cracked. "We have alerted the recovery team for transport to New Orleans. They will be on their way tonight."

About an hour before daylight, two Lear Jets landed at an abandoned World War II airstrip near the City of Algiers across the river from New Orleans. The pilots taxied up to a dilapidated old hangar, opened the side door of the plane and lowered the stairs. D'Angelo motioned for the men to follow him to the hangar where they would wait until they received orders from Star Gazer to move on the Center and kidnap Dr. Casstevens.

Chapter Three

V. J. strolled lazily through the throngs of night people and sightseers moving in and out of a hundred Quarter cabarets sipping Hurricanes, Sazeracs and Abita Amber Beer to the intoxicating sounds of cool to red-hot jazz and everything in between. He was physically present but emotionally absent for his mind was preoccupied with losing his job and all the ramifications of the most recent experiment. He approached the River Walk, where the longhaired gathered and spooked the normal folks, and sat down on a park bench to wait for Macee. He really could care less what any of the night people in the Quarter looked like and, besides, he knew they were harmless.

"I see a bad moon a'risin'," he sang, somewhat off key, as he looked at the full moon coming up over Algiers across the river. He ran his fingers through his matted salt-and-pepper hair and nervously stroked his three-day growth of beard as he tried to relax and enjoy the music and other sounds and excitement of the Quarter.

New Orleans is the most exciting city in America where it's carnival time all the time and a city where you can hide from the world and not be bothered. I hope Macee is on time. She's been late every night this week."

He glanced at the cruise boat Natchez moored nearby and could hear the Dukes of Dixieland playing "When the Saints Go Marching In."

"If she's not here in five minutes, I'm out of here. I'll just eat by myself."

"*Lesse les bantan roulez!* Let the good times roll!" Macee Marineaux shouted as she slapped V. J. on the back, almost knocking the breath out of him.

V. J. smelled her cheap perfume. "You're late. What time zone did you think I was talking about when I said eight o'clock?"

"I don't know. What you been doing?"

"Just hackin' around."

"I was looking forward to seeing you."

"Well, where you been?"

"Axe me," she said with a Cajun accent.

"Macee, it's not 'axe me' it's 'ask me'."

"That's what I said, 'axe me'."

"Okay, that's fine, but what kept you?"

She replied with a touch of sugar in her raspy voice. "*Fais-do-do*, I been in two street dances already tonight *Joie de vivre!*"

Macee Marineaux was a quadroon, a Creole of mixed Negro and French Canadian ancestry, who barely missed being pretty. She was a big double-jointed girl of ample proportion, over six-feet tall and bulged in a few of the wrong places, even though she was heavy into karate, Yoga and aerobics. Her mouth arched upward at the corners giving her a perpetual smile and she had long, black hair, a big brown pair of roving eyes and fiery-red fingernails.

V. J. knew she did not look like one of Charlie's Angels, but he liked hanging out with her. And she always amazed him when she walked into his apartment and yelled, "Ha—ya" a couple of times then kicked with her right leg and touched the eight-foot ceiling with her foot. But to V. J. the biggest problem with a quadroon like Macee is that every time she hears music her feet start to dance.

I've always heard that Creole women are supposed to be the most beautiful in the world. I guess Macee missed out on the beauty part. She's a little light on the dark side for a Creole. And she's always trying to live in the future before it ever arrives.

"Want to know something, V. J.?"

"What's that?"

"I've got a new karate instructor. His name is Peg-leg Pete. He's a black belt and one of the best teachers in New Orleans. Just has one leg."

"Would it be asking too much for you to tell me how a man with a peg leg can be a karate instructor?"

"No, he pivots on his good leg and then he hits you with his peg leg. No one in New Orleans can beat him."

"I see."

Macee smiled and touched V. J.'s arm. "I sent my mother a birthday card today. It said, "'To my second favorite parent from your second favorite daughter.'"

"That wasn't very nice."

"Well, I shoplifted the fanciest card I could find."

V. J. knew she had been married several times but she didn't talk much about it.

One day she said with a half-groan, half-sigh, "When I got pregnant my first husband told me working was out of the question. So he quit his job."

"I didn't know you had a baby."

"She's a little girl now and my mom's raising her down in Golden Meadow but when I get older I'm going to bring her to New Orleans."

"Macee, you're already thirty years old."

"My second husband was killed in a bungee-jumping accident in the Superdome. The man controlling the bungee cords miscalculated and he hit his head on the concrete floor."

She told V. J. her relationship with the bungee jumper was a two-way street and she got run over from both directions.

"When I divorced the undertaker – which was the third worst marriage of my life – the judge told me, 'Miss Marineaux, I've decided to give you $300 a month in alimony.'"

A broad grin creased her face. "My husband thanked the judge and said, 'I'll kick in a few bucks, too.' Made the judge so mad he threw him in jail for three days."

V. J. thought her story about the undertaker was funny but he was in no mood to laugh.

Macee frowned and squinted her eyes. "You know, V. J., you should never marry anyone until you get to know all about them. Sometimes they turn out to be boys trying to act like men."

"You're a regular Mecca for marital advice."

"My cousin is getting married next week – her name is Rhonda and she's a weight lifter, but the guys at the gym call her 'Wide Load' because she's a little hippy. She's marrying an ice cream peddler who drives one of those little Happy Time trucks up and down the street."

"That's real good."

"She outweighs him eighty pounds, but I don't guess that matters. May put some pepper in his gumbo."

"Yeah, maybe."

V. J. tried to analyze why he liked hanging out with a woman who always seemed locked in some kind of 1960s time warp. *She never met a loser she didn't like and perhaps that's why she likes to hang out with me.*

He knew she had more sanctity than most of the

parish priests in New Orleans.

If all her friends were to jump off a bridge, she wouldn't jump with them – she'd be at the bottom to catch them.

"Macee, let's go, I've been waiting for an hour and I'm hungry."

"Where we going, to the Rusty Nail again? I hate that place."

"No, it's too late for the Nail, I want some Chinese take out from Wimpy Wang's."

"I'd rather go to Barbecue Bob's – it doesn't gas you up as much as Chinese."

"Well go on and I'll meet you back at my place."

"Okay, it's Wimpy Wang's."

They picked up the takeout at Wimpy Wang's and walked out into the crowded Rue St. Philippe Street past graffiti-fouled walls toward his apartment building across from the old Postal Emporium.

"You know, V. J., those 'walk' and 'don't walk' signs are handy. They give the people of New Orleans something to read while they're jaywalking."

"Yeah, yeah."

Macee turned to V. J. with a solemn look on her face. "You guys at the Center kill monkeys, don't you."

"Sometimes."

"I heard about this pet monkey down on Toulouse Street that was working as a pickpocket for a gypsy fortuneteller. They made a lot of money 'till the gypsy got caught. Now he's in the slammer and I think animal control put the monkey to sleep. Poor thing, it wasn't his fault."

V. J. pushed on the wrought-iron gate that opened into a large courtyard where there were sculptured fountains and a *garconnier* with cottonwoods and crepe myrtles near a cloistered patio. Macee held on to the ornate iron banister, left to rust in careless neglect, as she followed him up the stairs to the balcony that was covered with hanging vines, cracked plaster on old bricks and paint peeling from the gray ceiling.

Macee opened the apartment door. "*Il pue dans! It stinks in here!*" She opened the windows facing Rue St. Philippe to let the place air out. "I can't eat nothing with this smell."

V. J. broke the chopsticks apart and began eating his sweet and sour pork. "Smells okay to me."

She opened the refrigerator and smelled the stale pizza and soured milk. "This place is dirty and V. J. you're a slob. You wear worn-out suit coats and dirty old Reeboks without socks. And you got coffee stains on your necktie, you smell like embalming fluid and your jeans don't look like they are going to stand another wash. How did you ever make a scientist?"

"Just hush, you're going to talk me into a rash. Why don't you go read the funny papers or something? I'm tired and hungry."

"*Mon cherie,* you're thirty-six and that's old enough to at least try to keep your apartment clean."

"Was I talking too fast for you when I said 'hush'? Now let me eat."

"Well you need to grow up and just remember, if you smell yourself, others have been smelling you for three days."

"Don't give yourself a headache worrying about it."

Macee opened the curtains. The light from the street sent shadows dancing up and down the walls of the apartment. She picked up the dishes from the beer-stained tablecloth on the kitchen table and his dirty clothes that were scattered from the living room to the bedroom. She glanced inside his study and saw all the books and old newspapers that covered the desk and most of the floor, and a cracked *jardiniere,* filled with waste paper, by his desk.

A cat wandered in the open door of the apartment and she heard it hiss as V. J. grabbed it and threw it off the balcony. "No good cats, no matter how high you throw them, they always land on their feet."

"Shame on you, poor cat. I thought you liked animals."

"Not cats."

"Now, I'm going to do the wash and you need to take a bath. Your deodorant called it quits several days ago and you smell just like this nasty apartment."

"Lifestyles of the rich and famous, and besides that, I've got a reputation to uphold."

"Please don't say that, this place is a wreck. There's green stuff all over the jambalaya and dirty rice and these Zatarains boxes are moldy."

He removed his Nike ball cap and scratched his head. "Who cares, the jambalaya was good and those are the leftovers and, besides, I like my apartment like it is and I never use deodorant."

Macee continued cleaning up the apartment. She turned to V. J. "Did you know you have to have a license to hunt, fish, drive a car or even to own a dog but anybody who wants to can run for president?"

"What you talking about, what's that got to do with anything?"

"I don't know; I was just studying on it."

"Well from now on try to keep those crazy thoughts to yourself."

Her face turned red. "If you don't quit talking so mean to me I'm out of here! Maybe I am a loser, but you're a loser, too, so chill!"

"Don't get your panties in a wad."

What's got into her?

He finished his Chinese food. "Now I'm going to watch the Korean midget wrestlers and maybe a monster movie."

He kicked the old black-and-white television set twice and the picture popped on.

"V. J., you want a cup of coffee and some olives or something?"

"Together, or separate?"

"Well, I guess separate but you could put them together."

He shook his head and tried to understand what she was saying. "No, not today."

She loaded his laundry into a basket. "You want to go to the track and run with me in the morning?"

"No, I don't run."

"Come on, it'll make you feel good."

"Was I stuttering when I told you 'no'?"

"My track coach in college said I was good, even wanted me try out for the Nationals in the one- and two-hundred meters, maybe even more."

"Like what?"

"The Olympics."

"You're telling me another tall tale. You weren't going to the Nationals or anywhere else."

"Why are you always puttin' me down?"

"Cause you're making up stuff?"

"I'm not either, in my freshman year at Southwestern over in Lafayette I won three out of four track meets in the one- and two-hundred meters and set two state records, and if you don't believe me you can check the *Louisiana Almanac,* because I'm in there."

"You're serious, aren't you?"

"Yeah, we were the Ragin' Cajuns."

"Well, it's a relief to know you can do something besides dance."

"Sure I can, I'm thirty years old but I'm still a good runner. You've always thought I was a nobody and even treat me like a nobody, but I'm somebody, maybe a little down on my luck right now, but a real somebody."

He continued watching the Korean midget wrestlers. "Okay, I understand."

Wonder why she never told me she was a runner, or maybe I just wasn't listening.

"V. J., some of us are going to the Astrodome tomorrow night to see the Saints. San Francisco is in town for a pre-season game. You want to go with us?"

"Naw, the Saints been playing like they never saw a football. Now leave me alone, I want to watch TV. By the way, can you go to the Center with me tomorrow morning? I need to clean out my office and check on Rufus."

"Okay, hot lips," she said under her breath. "What a downer, my best friend is lazy and has no dreams beyond today and no ambition for tomorrow and absolute zero romantic intentions."

She returned from doing the laundry an hour later and saw the monsters on TV eating Tokyo. V. J. was sound asleep. She hit him twice in the forehead. "Hello, is anybody there?" But she couldn't wake him.

She wrote him a note. "*Mon cherie,* give me a call when you come out of your coma. And I've been thinking a lot about it, suggest you don't go to the Center tomorrow. Jupiter is too close to the moon. *Dieu vous garde,* God keep you." But she knew he wouldn't listen to her so she would meet him there.

She went downstairs and stepped out into the street where another parade was getting ready to start immediately and last forever.

Chapter Four

The next morning V. J. put on the same clothes he had worn all week, hurried down the stairs to the street and walked briskly through the Quarter toward the Center, stopping only to get a cup of coffee from a street vendor.

Macee was waiting for him when he arrived.

"Hi, V. J., did you read my note?"

"Yeah, I read it."

"Well?"

"Well what?"

"You never listen to nobody."

"Just hush."

He pushed open the door, said good morning to the security guard, and walked down the hallway to the stairs to his office. "Now, let's check on Rufus."

He opened the cage and a chimp that looked like Rufus jumped up and down, threw his arms around V.J.'s neck, licked his face and put his head on his shoulder.

"Hmmm --- weird."

V. J. led the chimp into his office and set him down in a chair, wondering what had become of his old friend Rufus.

Macee patted the chimp on the head. "Where's Rufus?"

"I don't know, but I'm going to find out!" V. J. said angrily.

He tried not to think the unthinkable that one of the other scientists had taken the chimp away to the lab for a final experiment and placed another chimp in his cage. Heretofore he had been able to protect his old friend from the dangerous, and often life-threatening, experiments.

He returned the chimp to the cage, latched the screen door and ran upstairs to the second-floor lab with Macee close behind. "They're going to have hell to pay if they've done something to Rufus."

V. J. pushed open the swinging doors, charged into the lab and met Dr. Al Germaine, a cancer researcher.

He shoved the startled scientist up against the wall. "What have you done with Rufus? You know he's off limits!"

Germaine pushed V. J. away and began to straighten his necktie. "Casstevens, none of my people have gone near that drunken chimp so get out of my face!"

V. J. went into a rage and turned over tables, poured out a tray of instruments and smashed a computer monitor. A lab assistant called security and the Pinkerton guard escorted V. J. and Macee back to his office.

Star Gazer observed the entire incident and reported it to Culverwell. "Mr. C, I now have new evidence of a radical change in the chimpanzee on which Casstevens performed the experiment. Suggest you instruct the recovery team to grab the doctor immediately."

"Yes, Star Gazer."

After he cooled down, V. J. and Macee began cleaning out his desk and packing his personal things like the yellow rubber duck, the Green Hornet poster and a euchre deck of playing cards, well worn from hundreds of hours of playing solitaire to pass the time. There were also old magazines and newspapers and thousands of pages of computer printouts from aging research centers all across America and around the world stacked in piles beside his desk.

"V. J. this stuff is junk and you ought to throw it away. Just like a bachelor."

"In your dreams."

"When you carry it home all you're going to have is office junk piled on apartment junk, and that's not cool."

V. J. took another look at the chimp in the cage. "Macee, this chimp acts like Rufus and even looks like him but all the gray hairs are gone from around his mouth."

"*Voila,* maybe Rufus has been foolin' around with the girls and it's one of his sons."

"No, we don't let the chimps fool around." V. J. glanced at his watch. "It's lunch time. You hungry?"

"Yeah and this place is depressing. I wish I could turn the animals loose."

"Why not?"

He walked to the wine cabinet and moved it back away from the wall. Then he opened all the cages and led the chimps to the secret passage where Macee swatted them on their butts and sent them on their way. He turned all the dogs, cats, pigs and rabbits loose, and placed the white rats in a large box and carried them to the secret passage.

Macee saw the rats and screamed. V. J. laughed so hard he couldn't get his breath.

After all the animals were out of the building, V. J. pulled the wine cabinet back over the entrance, picked up the box of white rats, held his head up real high and whistled a tune as he and Macee followed the animals out into the bright sunlight. He had never felt better in his life.

At exactly twelve o'clock, a large brown commercial van carrying the ten-man recovery team pulled up in front of the Center. The men, dressed in army fatigues, wearing ski masks and carrying H & K automatic weapons equipped with silencers, jumped out of the back of the van and hurried to the front door.

The Pinkerton guard, who thought they were extras in a movie that was being filmed in the city, smiled and waved at them just as one of the men charged inside and hit him in the head with a blackjack. Then Frankie D'Angelo and several of his men ran down the stairs to the basement and into V. J.'s office. He cursed when he saw that V. J. was not there.

D'Angelo keyed his radio. "Team Leader to Star Gazer."

"Go ahead, Team Leader."

"We can't find the subject."

"Keep looking, he was in the building only minutes ago."

"Ten-four."

D'Angelo motioned to his men to follow him and they raced up the stairs to the second floor lab where they encountered Dr. Germaine and his assistants.

"Up against the wall!" D'Angelo barked. "Where is Casstevens?"

"We haven't seen him since this morning," Germaine replied.

Weegie Peabody screamed when two masked men barged into her office and ordered her and Dr. Townsend down to the second floor lab with the others.

D'Angelo and his men searched all the offices but could not find V. J. He keyed his radio and said, "Star Gazer, this is Team Leader, we still can't find the subject."

"Search the basement again, there's a secret passage in the back that he uses, maybe he's hiding in there."

D'Angelo found the passageway behind the wine cabinet but there was no sign of Casstevens. It was apparent they were not going to find him so they returned to the second floor lab.

D'Angelo fired several rounds from his automatic weapon into the ceiling and the women screamed. "Now, everybody down on the floor! Tie them up, hands behind their backs then let's get out of here!"

Suddenly, Weegie Peabody ran toward an open window and screamed. "Help, police, somebody help us, please help us!" Then she jumped headfirst out the window to the ground below. The other workers in the Center panicked and began throwing lab instruments, glass containers and books at the masked men.

Roscoe Chan broke the glass on the fire alarm, grabbed a fire axe and hit one of the masked men in the head splitting it wide open as blood from the wound spurted all over the floor.

D'Angelo and the others tried to defend themselves by hitting the lab workers with the butts of their automatic weapons. One of his men, who had been cornered by two of the lab assistants holding scalpels from a tray of instruments in their hands, killed both of them with a long burst from his automatic weapon.

The workers in the Center continued to scream, claw and scratch and Dr. Townsend hit one of the men up side of the head with a large ashtray, knocking him to the floor. D'Angelo shot Townsend twice in the chest then shot Germaine in the back as he tried to dial 911. Germaine staggered back away from the phone and fell to the floor, mortally wounded. Several ran out of the lab and down the stairs to get away from the masked men.

D'Angelo keyed his radio to the men guarding the entrance to the Center. "We've got hell up here, bodies scattered everywhere and some others are on their way down the stairs. Stop them now!" He heard muffled reports from their automatic weapons.

D'Angelo called Star Gazer again. "My boys have killed most of the people over here – maybe all of them."

"You had orders from Mr. C that there was to be no killing. The old man is going over the edge on this one."

"But I had to stop them or we'd all be on our way to jail."

"I've got everything on tape and I'll try to square things with Mr. C. Now get out of there!"

"What about Casstevens?"

"You've got his picture so wait till after dark then hit the streets of the French Quarter and find him and the big tall broad."

"Ten-four."

D'Angelo hand-signaled to his men to return to the van and they drove away. The entire caper lasted only twelve minutes.

V. J. and Macee strolled lazily along the River Walk enjoying the beautiful summer day when they met a young boy on roller blades who told them traffic was tied up all over the Quarter.

"Must be a hundred monkeys loose and dogs and rabbits. Someone said the zoo turned them loose."

V. J. smiled.

After lunch, he led Macee down toward the river to the secret entrance and on to his office and was startled when he saw his desk turned over and most of the papers and file folders scattered everywhere.

"Macee, look at this, the jerks have trashed my office!"

"*Mon dieu-que,* my goodness what happened?"

"I don't know, but let's check with security."

Macee followed him up to the foyer where they found five dead bodies on the floor and the guard in the blue uniform slumped down on his desk.

V. J. set the officer up in his chair. "What happened here?"

The guard gave him a glazed look then fell over dead.

They ran up the stairs to the second floor laboratory where they found Townsend, Germaine and the other dead workers. The walls were splattered with blood and there were automatic weapon shell casings on the floor.

Macee's face was pale. "We've got to call the police."

V. J. paced back and forth through the laboratory, now in ruins, in a daze.

Suddenly Macee screamed. "V. J., Dr. Townsend is still alive!"

V. J. rushed to where Townsend was lying in a pool of blood and cradled his head in his arms.

"What happened, Doctor?"

"They were looking for you, Casstevens."

"Oh, no."

"Yes, their leader asked where you were and we told him we didn't know. Now you get out of here right now and find a safe place to hide, they'll probably be coming back for you."

"I'm going to call an ambulance."

"Get away from here now and stay away! Lose yourself in the Quarter until the police arrive."

"Macee, bring him a drink of water."

She handed him a glass of water and he put it to Townsend's lips. But when he raised his head to drink he groaned, gasped for breath and died.

V. J. gently placed Townsend's head down on the floor. "Macee, we've got to get out of here!"

They ran back through the secret passage and out into the street where V. J. found a pay phone and called the police. "There's been a massacre at the National Research Center on Chartres! You need to get down there and quick!"

"Can you give us a little more information and who is this calling?" the desk sergeant asked.

"Just get down there now – a lot of people are dead!"

V. J. hung up the phone and felt something hugging his leg. He looked down and noticed it was one of the chimps from the Center, the one he had found in Rufus' cage.

"Hey, fella, where you been hiding out?" V. J. asked, taking the chimpanzee by the hand and leading him into the alley. "You know you do look a lot like Rufus."

The chimp threw his long arms around V. J.'s neck, kissed him and licked his face. When he backed away, he noticed a tattoo in the chimp's left ear, the number 444.

"Macee, look at this! The chimp has the number 444 tattooed in his left ear. That's the same number I gave Rufus several years ago."

"*Mon dieu-que!*"

Star Gazer had picked up V. J. and Macee when they first returned to the Center and found the dead bodies. He keyed his radio. "Star Gazer to recovery Team Leader."

"Leader, go," Frankie D'Angelo said.

"The subject found the dead bodies. He and a broad left through the secret passage."

"Ten-four, Star Gazer."

D'Angelo and the recovery team members ditched the brown van then changed back into street clothes. They rented two white Chevy Suburbans and returned to the hangar at the old abandoned airport near Algiers to plan their search for V. J. and Macee. Ten additional team members arrived from Chicago in a Culverwell jet that afternoon, giving D'Angelo twenty men for the search.

He motioned for his men to gather around an old table in the center of the hangar. "Now listen up, I want you to fan out across the French Quarter and find Dr. Casstevens and his girlfriend Macee Marineaux. We've been monitoring the police channel on our scanner and neither of their names has been mentioned at this point."

Then he passed out pictures of V. J. "The doctor may be with the broad or they could possibly have separated."

"Do we have pictures of the girl?" Healy John Hurt, one of the team members, asked.

"No, but we know she is a quadroon, over six feet tall with long brown hair."

D'Angelo took a map of the French Quarter from his briefcase and spread it out on the table. The men moved in close.

"The Quarter covers ten city blocks and there will be thousands of people there during the evening hours. We will key off of Bourbon Street – that's where I would go if I was on the lam. But I also want you to check the areas around Dauphine, Royal and Chartres running east and west and St Louis, Toulouse, Peters and Orleans, running north and south."

Then he gave each of the men a Motorola hand radio.

"I want you to form up in teams of two and go find Casstevens. And keep your radios on channel one. Any questions?"

There were none.

"Okay, let's rock and roll."

They boarded the Suburbans, returned to the French Quarter and began their search.

Chapter Five

Detective Lieutenant Scott Dula and Detective Charlie Francis, his young partner, arrived at the Center about 1 p.m.

"Okay, Mike, what you got?" Dula asked Sergeant Mike L'Enfant, the head of the patrol unit on the scene.

"Not much, Lieutenant. Fourteen dead and a jumper who broke both of her legs when she went out a second-floor window. My men are going door to door in the surrounding buildings to see if anyone saw or heard anything. It's sketchy, but it looks like this: a brown commercial van pulled up in front of the building, stopped and maybe a dozen armed men wearing camo outfits and ski masks jumped out the back of the van and ran into the Center."

"Yeah, go on."

"Several of the people who saw them thought they were extras in a movie being filmed in the city."

"Any license plate?"

"Yeah, one lady remembered the last four numbers on the plate, seven nine four three. But before we had a chance to run the numbers we got word that an abandoned brown van that fit the description was found at the airport."

"Stolen of course."

"Right, Lieutenant."

"Okay, get the forensic people out to the airport and go through the van and see what they can find. But

these guys are pros and I doubt if we turn up anything."

"Our people are on their way."

Dula and Francis entered the building and saw the
dead bodies in the foyer.

Jewel Fontnote, the head of the CSI unit for the New
Orleans Police Department, saw the lieutenant and mo-
tioned him to come over near the stairway. "Hi Scott,
Charlie. There are more bodies upstairs."

"Got any good news?" Dula asked.

"Not yet, it's really a bad scene, real bad. I've been
in this business for twenty-five years and have been
through serials and drive-bys and everything else but
I've never seen anything like this."

"Let's take a look," Dula said.

They walked up the stairs to the second floor laboratory and saw the other dead bodies scattered across the
room.

"Man, none of this makes any sense," Francis said.
"Could it have been terrorists?"

Dula saw bloody tracks all over the floor. "I know
one thing, Charlie, they were wearing *bata* boots, like
we wore in Nam." He pointed to a boot print in a pool
of blood. "But I guess you can buy them at any army
surplus store."

"We have found a few camo fibers which may have
come from the intruders, but we'll know more later,"
Jewel Fontnote said. "We're dusting for prints and
maybe we'll get lucky."

"Okay, Charlie, after we get back downtown, I want
you to interview the jumper that broke her legs and see
if she can give us any leads and find out if there was a
stash of drugs in the Center, maybe the kind you use on
animals."

"The EMT said the survivor is in bad shape and may not make it," Francis said.

"Just do what you can."

"Ten-four, Lieutenant."

Dula walked around the room and picked up several shell casings. He could tell from the marks of the firing pens they were from Nine Millimeter H and K automatic weapons.

"Got anything?" Jewel Fontnote asked.

"These come from high-dollar weapons, the kind Navy Seals carry."

"I see."

"Jewel, I want you to go over every inch of this building and I don't care if it takes a week, give me something."

"Okay, Scott."

"After you ID all the victims, try to find a roster to see if anyone is missing. I guess it could have been an inside job."

"Now there's something I want to show you."

She motioned for him to follow her downstairs to an office that looked like it had been trashed. Boxes and papers were scattered all around the room, the desk was turned over and all the file cabinet doors were open.

"They were looking for something down here," she said. "This is the only office in the building that was even touched."

"Can you tell whose office it was?"

"We've been through a lot of the papers on the floor and the name Casstevens keeps turning up. By the way, Lieutenant, we found three well-concealed video cameras in the cancer and AIDS research labs and one in this office. Someone was very interested in what was going on here."

"The boss may have been eavesdropping on his people. See if you can locate the monitor."

"The cameras were wireless and that means the monitor could be anywhere within a mile of the Center. But someone was watching the labs and this office."

"Okay Jewel, keep in touch. Everyone downtown, including the Mayor, wants something to tell the public. So let me know if you find anything."

"Ten-four."

"We've got to come up with something or it's going to be a long summer for the department."

On the way back downtown Dula tried to recap the events of the day.

"What have we got here? There's no apparent motive, no drugs in the Center, no stash of cash, it was almost like gangland-style killings."

"We've been called to the Center several times to put down animal rights demonstrations but I've never known those people to resort to violence," Francis said. "The people on the street couldn't tell us much just that the men wore camo and ski masks and everything came down do fast. Sergeant L'Enfant and his men are taking them all downtown for questioning and we'll keep trying."

"You know, Charlie, even after nearly thirty years with the department, I'm still shocked and surprised when lightning strikes."

"Yeah."

Scott Dula well remembered the day he joined the New Orleans Police Department, just a few weeks after he arrived home from Vietnam and was discharged by the Marine Corps. He knew that there was some kind of miracle involved in him becoming a cop, perhaps the result of the prayers of his mother, because when he was young he got in trouble with the law and had several misdemeanors and a felony on his record.

"At seventeen I was six-foot four, weighed two hundred eighty and played nose guard for the Loyola High School football team," he once told Francis. "Several sports magazines named me to the Schoolboy All-American team and, when I was a high school junior, colleges all across the land were sending scouts to see me play."

But he told the detective he also had a bad side. "I liked to walk into New Orleans bars and say, 'I'm Scott Dula, the toughest guy in town and I'll fight anybody in this rat hole!'"

There were always a few Cajuns or red necks that would fight him but he whipped them all and really enjoyed it.

Sometimes he wore an eye patch.

"Did you lose an eye?" a bartender asked him one night just before the fight began.

"No, the eye patch makes me look only half as bad."

Nature gave him thirty-two teeth but he had lost fourteen, mostly knocked out.

When he was a senior in high school he got into a fight and broke a couple of guys' jaws and was arrested. Judge Jackson Duplantier placed him on probation.

But in spite of his troubled past, several colleges, including LSU in Baton Rouge, wanted to recruit him to play football. His probation officer told him he could not go out of state to play ball because he wanted to keep an eye on him. So he went to LSU.

During his sophomore year, the Associated Press named him to the first-string All American and it appeared that he had a very promising, and lucrative, career ahead of him in the NFL.

But he couldn't stop fighting. One night he went into another bar and yelled, "I'm Scott Dula, anybody want to fight?"

His bravura backfired that night. A logger from the bayou country who was bigger than Dula stood up and hit him one time and he staggered back. Then he picked up a chair and hit the big logger and split his head open.

The bartender called the police and they arrested him and charged him with public brawling and assault and threw him into jail. His fight and subsequent time in jail was big news in Baton Rouge and all over the state.

The next day the LSU athletic director booted him off the team, much to the disappointment of the coaching staff.

As bad luck would have it, he went before Judge Duplantier's court again. When his name appeared on the docket, the judge stared at him for a long time. Then he lectured him for ten minutes on what a sorry human being he was and called him a bully and a troublemaker and said he ought to lock him up in jail and throw away the keys.

"You think you're the prize bull out there, don't you boy?"

"Yeah, something like that," Scott mumbled.

"Speak up boy!"

"Yes Sir."

"Okay, that's better."

Then the judge surprised everyone. "Mr. Dula, I still see some hope for you."

Scott raised his head slowly and looked directly at

the judge.

"I'm going to offer you a deal. You can either do a year in the Orleans Parish Jail or join the United States Marine Corps where they might be able to make a man out of someone as sorry and no good as you are. What will it be?"

Scott's attorney whispered in his ear. "Take the deal."

"Your honor, I would like to join the Marines."

The judge instructed a probation officer to make sure Scott went to the Marine Corps Recruiting Office that day.

Scott walked into the office to sign up for the Marines and saw a poster that said: "The Sky Is Blue, the Grass Is Green, Get Off Your Butts and Join the Marines."

After boot camp he was assigned to the First Marine Division and served with distinction in Vietnam. He re-upped twice and during three tours of duty he was promoted to sergeant and became something of a legend in the Corps as a tough jungle fighter.

One day Captain Andrew Call, his company commander, sent word for Scott to come to his hooch and told him they had a problem. The Marine major in charge of supply for some reason didn't like the captain and refused to give him and his men the supplies they needed. He wondered if Sergeant Dula had any ideas.

"Yeah, Capn' Call, I'll take care of it for you."

That night Scott and a couple of his buddies went to the morgue on the base at Da Nang. They found a dead Viet Cong in a black rubber body bag and cut off his hand. Then they went to the supply major's hooch and tied the hand to the light string. The major returned to his quarters half drunk and reached for the light switch.

He felt the hand, evacuated his bowels and fainted. When he woke up he found a note tied to the string. It said, "If A Company, First Marines don't get our supplies, the next hand will be yours."

Captain Call and his men received all of their supplies the next morning.

But there was also a downside in the war in Vietnam for he later told friends he buried enough good young men to qualify as an undertaker and he remembered those men every day.

After four years he decided to leave the Marines.

The day he was honorably discharged he learned that because of his service in the Corps, Judge Duplantier ordered all his arrest records expunged. That opened the door for him to apply for entrance into the New Orleans Police Academy. He was accepted and his sins never came back to haunt him.

He graduated with honors, joined the Police Department and was assigned to the French Quarter beat as a rookie cop. He was still there ten years later.

One day he met Judge Duplantier who was strolling through the Quarter during a lunch break. They exchanged pleasantries and Dula said, "A lot of people didn't think I could make it. But that was a whole lot of juice. I owe you."

The Judge smiled.

Police Chief John David Landry noticed Scott's work when he busted a woman cop who shot her partner who caught her breaking into stores down in the Quarter late at night. She shot him right through the temple.

Dula was the first officer on the scene.

The homicide detective assigned to the case checked her service revolver and found that it hadn't been fired. But Dula saw a small-caliber revolver she carried in her boot.

Dula called the detective aside. "You need to check her back-up pistol in her boot."

The detective found the other gun and discovered it had been fired. He guessed the ballistics would confirm it was the gun that killed her partner.

He read her Miranda rights. "Cuff her, Scott."

She screamed like she had been hijacked by a Klingon and fought Scott and cursed like a crazy woman. "I'm going to kill you, Dula. Watch your back because you'll see me coming for you one of these days."

Ballistics proved her gun killed her partner. A judge sentenced her to life in prison without parole.

After he solved the high-profile murder case involving a police officer, the other police officers put a sign on the door of his locker at the station that said: "New Orleans, Where You Get Mugged By Strangers And Murdered By Friends."

A year later, Chief Landry promoted him to detective and he gradually rose through the ranks to lieutenant. He was a tough cop with the reputation for fairness and everyone knew he was an untouchable and they respected him for it. And he no longer went into bars to pick fights. The other detectives gave him a plaque he kept on his desk that said: "Semper Fi Means You Got Holes in Your Shorts."

Through the years rookie cops often came to him for help when the job got too big for them and they were all stressed out and about to go over the edge. He advised the rookies, "Don't take life too seriously, it's not permanent."

"Charlie, I want you to check with NIH in Atlanta and get some idea of what kind of research they were doing at the Center," he said as his journey into the past came to an end.

The detective nodded.

CHAPTER SIX

V. J. felt caught between two fires and burned by them both as he, Macee and the chimp disappeared into the crowds of tourists and revelers moving in and out of the Quarter. He kept looking over his shoulder hoping no one was following them and winced when anyone brushed against him.

After wandering around the Quarter for an hour, he took Macee's hand and led her into a nearby alley where they hid in the shadows.

"Now Macee, we're in big trouble and you need to help me work through this thing and don't go crazy on me."

"Okay, but I'm scared, all those people getting killed and everything."

"Yeah, it was tragic and, before he died, Townsend said the killers would come looking for me."

"You know, he was trying to help you."

"Now we need a plan to stay alive. I can't call the police because I may be a suspect in the killings."

"Why, you didn't do anything."

"I know, but I was the only one who wasn't there when the others were killed and that would automatically make me a suspect."

V. J. flinched when a wino emerged out of the shadows and tapped him on the shoulder.

"Say Mack, did you know your little boy looks just like a monkey. And could you spare a couple of bucks to help an old man get something to eat?"

V. J. handed him five dollars and the man staggered off down the alley.

Macee smiled. "That was very nice helping the old man. Now, what are we going to do?"

"Try to stay alive."

"Well I'm not going to stay alive very long if I don't get something to eat."

"We can't eat now, we've got to keep moving. Let's split up. It'll be much safer. I'll take the chimp and meet you on the River Walk just before midnight."

"Well I don't want to split up. I'm scared and want to go back to my apartment."

"Whoever killed the people at the Center are going to be looking for me and they probably know we hang out together. So you can't go to your apartment. Just walk around the Quarter for a few hours and stay in the big crowds and don't dance in the streets and draw attention to yourself."

"Okay, but I don't like this one bit."

"You'll be fine."

"Could I have a hug just in case I never see you again?"

"Sure." He drew her close to him and kissed her on the cheek.

"That's the worst kiss I ever had. I've got two lips, you know."

V. J. led the chimp through the Quarter toward Bourbon Street which was choked with thousands of pleasure seekers who had left their morals in the hotel rooms and were roaming restlessly in and out of the honky-tonk bars, strip joints and tattoo parlors seeking artificial thrills.

There are enough people bumping into me to start an

earthquake, barkers, strippers, drifters, drunks, hookers. Welcome to the Queen City on the Mississippi.

He walked past the Blue Angel Club to an alley where he saw a drunk with no legs, his clothes ragged and stained with vomit, who had fallen down on the street. He picked him up and wiped his face with a handkerchief. Then he hailed a taxi. "Take him to the rescue mission over on Toulouse." He handed the driver ten bucks.

A few minutes later he returned to Bourbon Street where he joined the revelers that lined both sides of the street to see another parade, which was not the first, and would not be the last, of the night.

"It's party time!" a fat trumpet player, the leader of the parade, yelled as he danced around like he was getting ready to switch magnetic fields. The crowds applauded the trumpet player whose cheeks were bulging out like a couple of cheap rubber balloons about to pop and whose lips looked like they could blow up a tire.

A trombone player wearing a top hat and a lean, tall tuba player, joined him and the three of them danced in the street and and drove the crowd crazy. Dancing dogs, doing flips in the center of the street, trotted along behind the trio, followed by a menagerie of psychics with blue hair. A couple of teenagers stopped at the street corner to tap dance for quarters, never disturbing the old wino passed out on the sidewalk.

Along came the Mighty Midgets Rhythm and Blues Band, a half-dozen fire-eaters and a horse-drawn carriage filled with gypsy fortunetellers. The parade passed on down Bourbon Street with hundreds of revelers dancing in the streets as the crowds moved deeper into the Quarter.

V. J. and the chimp walked around the Quarter for

three hours. He ducked into a dark alley where he sat down to rest. He glanced at his watch and saw it was almost time to meet Macee. He rested for fifteen minutes then returned to the crowded streets and walked briskly toward the Market Café and up the stairs to the promenade on the River Walk, carefully looking over his shoulder every few seconds to make sure he was not being followed. From the River Walk he could see all the people on the street below, mostly wide-eyed tourists, listening to a black jazz band playing "Chinatown, My Chinatown" and drinking espresso and cappuccino.

Across the street he saw a purple-haired old man reading tarot cards at his table set up in the shadow of the Cathedral of St. Louis. Close by a street palm reader, with a golden earring, promised a clear look into the future for a buck fifty.

A gray-bearded old man, surrounded by a dozen tourists sitting on age-worn wooden benches, sang "There Is a Rose in Spanish Harlem," accompanied by a midget playing an electronic harmonica. White-faced mimes enchanted little children with the mystique of their body and facial movements endemic to the genre. Street barkers and assorted freaks and sycophants worked the crowd selling everything from tattoos to a kind of Love Potion Number Nine.

Quarter revelers gathered around an artist, a middle-aged man who looked like a pimp dressed in biker skins. He turned out charcoal portraits every fifteen minutes for five dollars a drawing.

A mulatto tour guide, a hint of mystery in his voice, explained to a group of sorority girls from Ole Miss over in Mississippi that the Quarter once was the home of Creoles, pirates, madams and voodoo queens like Marie Laveau.

"Minstrels and tellers of tales still write and sing ballads about the city's raucous and haunted past," the guide explained. "Restless ghosts, earthbound and doomed, still form the legendary gothic underground in the Quarter."

The girls giggled and squealed and anxiously waited for the witching hour when they would visit Marie Laveau's burial vault. Their guide told them she often appears through the mists and mysteries of old New Orleans accompanied by her one-eyed snake and three-legged dog, her constant companions.

"Marie is entombed in one of New Orleans walled cities of the dead surrounded by vaults, obelisks and monuments and some people of the night say her groans and screams can still be heard invading the quiet of her tomb."

V. J. knew he should keep moving. He led the chimp along the promenade where he could see the lights of Algiers across the river. Then the thing he feared most came on him when a stranger tapped him on the shoulder and stuck a gun in his ribs. "Dr. Casstevens, we'd like for you to come with us."

He turned around and saw two big and muscular men. The one with the gun took him by the arm. "We don't want any trouble so please do as we say."

V. J. began to tremble . "What's this all about?"

"You'll know soon enough," one of the men replied.

The other man keyed his hand radio. "Team Seven to Team Leader."

"Go, Team Seven."

"We have the subject."

"What's your twenty?"

"On the River Walk near Decatur."

"Stand by, I'm ten-two-five your twenty, ETA ten

minutes."

"Ten-four."

The man with the gun prodded V.J. toward a bench where he told him to sit down.

"Who are you guys?" V. J. asked.

Neither of the men replied.

Suddenly Macee walked up behind the two men and chopped one of them in the neck with her hand, then spun around and kicked the other man in the groin and both of them fell down on the wooden walkway.

"Come on, V. J., let's get out of here!" she shouted as she ran down the steps of the River Walk into the street, with V. J. and the chimp close behind. They didn't stop running until they reached Jackson Square on Chartres then hurried into the alley behind St. Ann Street where they stopped to catch their breath.

Macee gasped for breath. "That was a close one."

"Yeah, you saved us and I owe you."

"Maybe I'm not such a loser after all."

"No, you're not a loser." He reached over and gave her a big hug. "Now we need to keep moving."

As they walked through the crowded streets, Macee said, "I've got an idea."

"I don't need an idea."

"Might help keep us safe."

"What you talking about?"

"Mimes."

"Say what?"

"You know, mimes, like down in the Quarter."

"So?"

"There's a novelty shop called Wooly G's over on Poydras and in the back there's this makeup man who does nearly all the mimes in the Quarter. And he's good, too."

"Like how?"

"One night I saw one of his mimes over on Bourbon Street and I thought he was a statue till' he winked at me and I nearly fainted."

"Macee, you may have something, we could get made up like mimes and it would be a good cover."

"So you like the idea?"

"Yeah, I like it."

They hurried across the street and down a back alley toward Poydras Street to Wooly G's Show and Tell House of Novelties. They entered the front and walked to the back of the building and watched the makeup man put the final touches on a big, tall mime. After he finished, he said, "That'll be fifty bucks."

"You're next, lady." He motioned for Macee to sit down in his barber's chair. "Anything special?"

"No, just the white face and some rouge, lipstick and eye shadow."

The makeup man applied a crème foundation to her face and smoothed it with his fingertips. "This is the ultimate masquerade for Halloween, *Mardi Gras* or costume affairs. Tonight we will use the clown white light foundation for, I presume, you are a mime."

"Yes I am."

The makeup man took a powder puff and a sponge applicator and dusted her face with white powder several times until it was completely covered. "And would you like a little *La Femme* sparkle dust?"

"That sounds good."

Finally he added the eye shadow with an eyebrow pencil, lip color from a tube of lipstick and rouge.

"*Voila!*" He spun her around in the chair so she could see herself in the mirror.

"That's excellent, thank you."

"We have red, white and blue wigs on sale at the front desk. Next."

V. J. sat down in the chair. "Can you make me look like the Little Tramp, you know, Charlie Chaplin?"

"Whatever floats your boat but aren't you a little big for that?"

"Yeah, but let's do it."

The makeup man applied the foundation crème with a sponge, dusted it several times with white powder, added a little mustache and lots of eye liner and said, "Be right back."

V. J. watched him as he went to the front of the store then returned with a black derby and cane.

"Here's your hat and cane, just like the Little Tramp. That's fifty bucks each and another twenty for the hat and cane."

V. J. handed him the money and on their way out bought a red wig for Macee and two pairs of white gloves. He also bought a Zorro mask and hat for the chimp.

They walked out into the street. "Macee, let's split up and meet back right here at exactly 3 a.m."

"Okay, V. J., don't get lost."

"Yeah, and you be careful. I'll take the chimp with me."

V. J. mingled with the crowds the rest of the evening, often stopping to entertain children by pretending to unscrew the lids off of bottles, holding infants in his arms so their parents could get pictures and walking up and down the streets like a wooden soldier.

When he and the chimp approached the corner of Bourbon and St. Peters Streets, V. J.'s heart nearly quit him when he saw two men stopping tourists, showing them pictures. The tourists shook their heads. He walked over to the men, did a couple of Charlie Chaplin Little Tramp routines and held out a cup. One of the men put a couple of dollars in the cup. "Hey, clown, you seen these people around the Quarter anywhere?"

V. J. looked at the picture and nearly fainted. It was a picture of him. He smiled at the men, shook his head, did another Little Tramp routine and walked away.

D'Angelo keyed his hand radio and said, "Recovery team to Star Gazer."

"Star Gazer, go."

"One of our teams found Casstevens but he got away."

"He got away? What do you mean he got away?"

"My two men said they were attacked by a mob and the subject got away."

"Mr. C is not going to like this."

"Yeah, I know."

"Well, keep looking."

"We've crisscrossed the Quarter half a dozen times and there are wall-to-wall people all over the place. We've checked every bar and restaurant two, three times."

"Check them all again."

"Ten-four."

CHAPTER SEVEN

At 3 a.m. V. J. and Macee met back at Wooly G's House of Novelties.

"How'd it go, Macee?"

"Had a lot of fun, maybe when this is all over I may try being a mime for a while, made forty bucks. How about you?"

"One close call, did a Little Tramp routine for a couple of guys who were showing some pictures to tourists, pictures of me."

"Why'd you have to go and tell me that, I'm already scared."

"Yeah, me too."

"Where we going to spend the night? I really want to go back to the apartment?"

"No, not tonight, it's too dangerous, they'll be looking for us there for sure. I think we should go to the St. Louis Cemetery, we'll be safe there."

"You've got to be kidding! The cemetery? I'm already scared to death and you're taking me to the cemetery? That place is haunted."

"No, it's not haunted, that's just tour guide talk."

"It's not either, people have seen ghosts running all over that place."

"Just come on."

He took the chimp by the hand and walked through the alley toward the old St. Louis Cemetery as Macee reluctantly tagged along. Although there was a heavy fog and the Cemetery was spooky with its dark legends in America's most haunted city, V. J. knew it would be a good place to hide. He had visited the Cemetery a dozen times and was fascinated with the above-the-ground tombs and the myths that breed incestuously in a city heavily infected by superstition.

They walked through the gate past legendary vaults, obelisks and monuments, and the graves of creoles, pirates and voodoo queens like Marie Laveau. He heard she was vicious, malevolent and spiteful and those were her good points. *This is like a walled city of the dead. Some even say the place is crawling with the ghosts of gods and saints crying out for a final incarnation.*

"Mon dieu – que, I hate this place, can't we go to a motel?" Macee asked, her lips quivering as though she was about to meet Count Dracula or some other nut that bays at the moon.

Then she eased up real close to V. J. and put her arm around his waist. "We must be just this side of crazy to spend the night in a scary place like this."

"The whole world is a great big scary place."

"But not as scary as this graveyard."

"Just hush, we'll be safe here. Don't you Creoles say *sans souchi* or not to worry?"

"Well my friend told me you can hear the screams of madmen and tortured souls that are buried here. He said being out here is like reading secrets from the book of the dead. And what are we going to do if the police come looking for us?"

"I don't know, I haven't talked to the psychic hotline today."

"Well you need to do something. What if some little furry night visitors come by saying, 'Hi there, remember us?' Gee, sometimes I wish I was invisible but nobody can be invisible."

"There won't be any little night visitors and even if you were invisible you'd still bug the daylights out of me."

V. J. had heard the stories of ritual drumming and chanting in the midst of the sarcophagi splendor and the graphic tales of debauchery, blood lust and torture, but he never paid much attention to them. To him they were just myths of gothic horrors, folklore and Halloween mutations.

"V. J., you believe in God?"

"Yeah, I guess so. You believe?"

"Not since I was a little girl down in Golden Meadows and went to the Catholic Church every Sunday, but I didn't like church that much."

"My Mama was a Presbyterian."

"What's a Presbyterian?"

"I don't know, they build big churches and drive big cars."

"The priest at my church said that Jesus came down off the cross and was buried behind a big rock. Do you believe that?"

"I don't know, I wasn't there."

"Well that would really be something. Did you ever join the church?"

"No, I didn't want to be a Presbyterian or anything else because you couldn't drink or cuss, so I never did."

"What did your mama say about Jesus after they buried him behind the rock."

"She said that three days later he came back to life and then after that he returned to heaven."

"Radical, man. And if that's true he may be up there looking down at us right now, may have been watching us for years."

"Yeah, I guess it's possible and I reckon God won't go away just because you don't believe he's there."

"We better watch what we do or he's going to get us real good."

"Maybe not, Macee, those Presbyterians say that God is good and wants to be our friend."

"Well, if he's up there somewhere looking at us to-night sure, I'll be his friend."

V. J. was not the least bit superstitious but sometimes wondered if at times some exiled god had returned to New Orleans to take up his throne and rig the rules so that he or no one else could win.

The universe sure gets sideways now and then. You come into this world alone and you die alone and everything in between in transient with echoes all around us like we're adrift in a sea of illusion. But the only deities we ever see are the pseudo-gods in black robes. First we control the gods, then the gods control us. If we keep foolin' around with the false gods we might make the real God mad. I wish the real God would appear and tell us it's all over and the good guys have won and our good luck means that bad luck has gone away forever.

"Macee, you know life is such a mystery and I don't know where I came from, what I'm doing here or where I'm going when I die. I'm just not programmed to give an intelligent answer."

Surely life was made for something better than this. I would blame all my problems on the blackbirds in a dead and rotting tree if I thought it would help, especially when hell seems to have me by the throat. Or blame it on a phantom witch coming to settle an old account on a night like this, in a fog like this.

There in the Cemetery he sensed a mystical presence. At first it startled him then as flashes of the past raced through his mind he felt a strange calm. *Maybe I need to give myself another chance. The past is a lingering nightmare, a closet door forever ajar and you can paint it vivid, paint it sad, it's there and somehow I must learn to live with it.*

That night with Macee and the chimp, his only two friends by his side, he decided that when a man runs from himself he has a long way to go and he wondered if he was still waving sadly at a parade that had long since passed him by. *Maybe Macee is right after all when she says it's a long, long way from now to somewhere.*

Macee squealed like she'd just heard the devil call her name. "*Poo-yie*! I heard something, over by that big white vault!"

V. J. walked over to the vault and saw an old wino who apparently fell off the vault where he was trying to sleep.

"We've got to get out of here, it's not safe," Macee said. "What if we see the troubled spirits they say live here and the howlings? They are tortured with madness and go around whispering death."

"We're not going to hear the howlings, now just lay down and try to get some sleep."

"What about the crying woman?"

"What about her?"

"Some bad guys took her children and killed them and people say you can hear her roaming through this Cemetery crying and searching for them."

"Macee, just hush."

"Huh uh, they say she is tormented by an angry spirit and has a conscience crying out for absolution and a witch wakes her up each morning."

"Go to sleep."

"I can't sleep and you could be a little more understanding of the way I feel."

"I can only please one person a day and today ain't your day. And, what's more, tomorrow ain't looking too good, either."

"If you loved me would you still love me when I'm old and gray? Which will probably be at the end of this week."

"Macee, please."

"What if we meet up with some grave robbers?"

"We won't meet any grave robbers."

"V. J., what color do you dream in?"

"Who cares, now let me get some rest."

Neither of them slept much during the night and just before sunup V. J. stood up, yawned and stretched his arms. "Okay, let's go back to the Quarter."

They found a newsstand and picked up a copy of the *Times-American* newspaper. The banner headline said: "Fifteen Dead in National Research Center Massacre." The article was based on an interview with Chief of Police John David Landry.

"This is the worst act of violence in New Orleans history," the Chief said. "'We have turned up no solid evidence or motive for the killings but believe the members of some gang may have brazenly entered the Center looking for drugs. Meanwhile, Detective Lieutenant Scott Dula has been assigned to investigate the killings and to work with the government agencies to try to find out exactly what happened at the Center and determine who is responsible."

The article also quoted Lieutenant Dula. "We are looking for a survivor by the name of Victor Casstevens and have asked anyone who knows his whereabouts to contact the Police Department."

"Macee, the police have found nothing but they are

looking for me."

V. J. continued reading the article, and several related sidebars. One said that Weegie Peabody, the director's secretary, broke both of her legs when she jumped out of the second-floor window and is in critical condition.

"Macee, we need to find a telephone."

They walked up the alley to a phone booth on Dauphine Street where he dialed the Police Department.

"I would like to speak to Lieutenant Scott Dula."

"Yeah, you and half the people in New Orleans," a haughty desk sergeant with a husky voice replied.

"Tell him it's V. J. Casstevens."

"Stand by and I'll patch you through to his car. Car thirty-three, this is central."

"Go ahead central."

"We have a V. J. Casstevens on the line, wants to talk to you."

"I'll talk to him, patch him through." Dula motioned to Francis to call central on his cell phone and put a trace on the call.

"Yeah, Dula."

"This is Casstevens."

"Dr. Casstevens, I'm sure you've heard about the tragedy at the Center."

"Yes, I'm the one who called it in yesterday."

"Well, we'd really like for you to come downtown and answer a few questions."

"I have no knowledge of what happened. I wasn't there."

"I'd really like for you to help us clear this up." Dula wanted to keep him on the line long enough for the trace.

However, Macee, who was timing the call, told V. J. to shut it down.

"I'll call you again this evening after I've had some time to think." V. J. hung up the phone.

"Did we get him, Charlie?" Dula asked.

"That's a negative."

"He's a smart one, knew exactly when to cut us off."

V. J. and Macee were both tired and worn out so he decided to rent a room where they could get some rest.

"Macee, I want you to get us a room at the Prince Conti, just around the corner." He handed her his last three twenty-dollar bills. "Give the clerk some weird name since those guys, whoever they are, may be looking for you, too."

"Don't say that, it scares me. I don't want anybody looking for me. I just want to forget all of this and have some fun roaming around the Quarter and watching parades with my friends."

"You're irritating the fire out of me and it's only eight o'clock in the morning."

"Is this all the money you've got? Maybe you need to go to the bank."

"I'm into the banks so deep now they think there's been a stick-up. We'll have to use credit cards, even though they can be traced."

About thirty minutes later, Macee returned to the alley and said they had room 420 at the Prince Conti.

"It's a hundred a night."

"Okay, I guess we can scrape that up."

He walked around the corner to an ATM and drew out forty more dollars.

They decided to mingle with the crowds and continue their mime routines until noon, then go to the room. And they carefully watched for anyone suspicious following them.

Macee went to the hotel first and, when she saw it was safe, called V. J. at a pay phone near the alley.

The phone rang and V. J. picked up the receiver. "Yeah."

"It's me, and the coast is clear."

He hung up the phone, went around to the back of the Prince Conti and he and the chimp climbed up the fire escape stairs to the fourth floor where he pried open a window and climbed through it into the hallway. He knocked on the door to room 420. Macee opened it and let them in.

V. J. switched on the television to hear the noon news but there was a commercial with a guy wearing a 1930s straw hat, a sharks-skin suit and dancing with a cane. "Car wreck, hurt your back, need a lawyer, call Cadillac Jack."

"Dumb commercials."

The killings at the center was the top story as the blow-dried anchor man said, "Police are still looking for a break in the National Research Center murders and, as of news time, there are no substantive leads in the case, according to Lieutenant Scott Dula who is leading the investigation. Now we go live to Police Headquarters where Lieutenant Dula is standing by.

"Lieutenant, have you turned up any leads in this horrendous case?"

"We've been unable to establish a motive and our forensic work is still incomplete, so we're hoping to get a break in the next day or two."

"We've heard rumors that one of the scientists at the Center, a Dr. Victor Casstevens, is missing and may be implicated in the murders."

"We are looking for Dr. Casstevens and would like

to ask him a few questions, but no, he is not a suspect at this time."

"Lieutenant, we've also heard that there was some top-secret research going on at the Center, could the murders be related to that research?"

"I don't have anything to say on that matter, but when we turn something, we'll let you know."

"There you have it, our interview with Lieutenant Scott Dula, and we'll keep you informed as further events unfold. Meanwhile, here is a picture of Dr. Cas-stevens and if you have seen this man please contact the New Orleans Police Department."

V. J. nearly soiled his underwear when the TV station flashed his picture on the screen.

"Macee, come here, they've got my picture on TV."

"Yeah, you look real good."

"Don't say that, everybody will be looking for me and will know what I look like."

"But it's a real good picture and an honor being on TV."

"Ok, just forget it."

She went to bed and soon was sound asleep but V. J. walked the floor and worried the rest of the day as the horrendous events of the past twenty-four hours flashed through his mind.

Why were all the people at the Center killed? Why was my office the only one that was ransacked? And why does this chimp have a 444 tattooed in his left ear? That's bizarre.

A couple of hours before dark he dropped off to sleep but the chimp awakened him licking his face.

"Stop it, that's nasty," he scolded, swatting at the chimp jumping around the room. "Just like Rufus."

Then he thought the unthinkable. Could it be Rufus?

Suddenly he remembered that Rufus had two toes

cut off of his left foot and decided to check him out.

The chimp was cutting up, careful not to get too far away from V. J. Every few minutes he would jump into his lap, kiss and slobber all over him, then start playing again.

V. J. grabbed the chimp and held him long enough to check his left foot. Two toes were missing. The chimp wiggled free and ran around the room, jumping up and down and swinging from an old light fixture hanging from the ceiling.

He walked over to the bed and shook Macee. "Wake up, this is awesome."

She rubbed her eyes. "*Excusez-moi,* what you talking about?"

"This chimp has two toes missing on his left foot, just like Rufus."

"So?"

"Well, I think it's strange, and the tattoo."

"Those chimps all look alike to me, *mon cherie.* They stink and do as they please and pee all over everything whenever they get ready."

V. J. was confused but knew he had to find some answers.

That evening he called his friend Tito Markentel at the Louisiana State University Med School Laboratory.

"Tito, here."

"This is V. J."

"Don't call me, man, every cop in New Orleans is looking for you."

"Chill out, Tito, it's okay, I need a favor." He could tell that Tito was really poppin' his rivets.

"Not in this lifetime, you're too hot to fool with, all those people getting killed."

"Yeah, well that's what this is all about. I need a

DNA test run tonight."

"No way, man, I'm not foolin' with anything you got."

"Tito, it's life or death."

"Yeah, your life, and maybe my death."

"No, man, nobody will ever know. I'll send Macee over to your place with a blood sample. She'll be there in an hour."

"I don't know."

"It's important to me and you remember I put you up for three months after your wife ran off with that chiropractor who had been giving her adjustments."

"Hey, that's not fair, we're talking about gangland killings and throats gettin' cut."

"Please, Tito, can I send Macee over?"

There was a long pause on the line then Tito sighed. "Okay, tell her to come on."

"Thanks, Tito, I'll dance at your wedding."

"Just send flowers to my funeral."

"By the way, do you still have the blood samples from the tests we did on all the chimps last year?"

"Yeah, on the computer."

"Okay, I'm sending you another sample and I want to know if you can get a match on it."

"Okay, but after this we're even and I don't want to ever see or hear from you again. A guy could get killed foolin' around with you."

"Okay, Tito."

V. J. sent Macee to a nearby pharmacy to pick up several small syringes. When she returned, he drew blood from the chimp's arm, wrapped the syringe in a towel and handed it to Macee to take to Tito Markentel.

He paced back and forth in the room as he waited for her to return with the results from the DNA test.

About midnight there was a rap on the door. He looked through the peephole and when he saw it was Macee opened the door. "What you got?"

"Well, Tito says he doesn't know what the excitement is all about. It's a perfect match with 444."

V. J. felt faint and had to sit down to keep from passing out. All the pieces of the puzzle suddenly began to fit together and now he realized why the people at the Center had been murdered.

I may have found the magic bullet and some very unsavory people know about it. Apparently that last experiment on Rufus has significantly reversed his aging process.

V. J. paced the floor but Macee went into the bathroom, pulled off her clothes and slid into the tights she carried around in her purse. Then she returned to the bedroom to do her yoga exercises.

She sat down on the floor and breathed deeply.

"V. J. come on and do the *asanas* with me. The postures will quiet your body and put your mind at ease."

"That's just a bunch of foolishness, now hush, I'm trying to think."

"It will tighten up your cheeks."

"My cheeks are just fine."

"Well the *asanas* are no more foolish than you trying to find some way for people to live halfway forever. Besides, it will help you make peace with your higher self."

"I don't want to make peace with my higher self."

He looked at her with her ankles clasped behind her neck.

"Now watch me, V. J., I'm going to touch my nose with the tip of my tongue. It does wonders for the neck muscles. Actually, licking your nose isn't a particularly attractive ability. I'd rather be able to play the clarinet. I mean, even if people knew that you could lick your nose with your tongue, it's nothing you would ever be called on to do at parties, even dull parties. But they might want you to play the clarinet."

"That's real good, Macee."

"Want me to do a body scan and listen to your rhythms."

"No body scan, not tonight."

CHAPTER EIGHT

Alexander Culverwell looked out the window of his penthouse at the Chicago skyline and cursed the fate that had caused his health to fail. Although *The Chicago Herald* recently published a list of the wealthiest men in the city and he was at the top of the list, with a fortune of billions of dollars, it didn't mean a thing to a man who was living, and dying, in a wheelchair.

Money is nothing and there will be no armored cars hauling my assets to the cemetery when I die. I have everything and I have nothing. And I'm growing weaker every day.

He turned his wheelchair and went to his communications center, an adjacent room filled with dozens of computers, phone lines and TV monitors, the nerve center for his network that monitored aging research throughout the world.

Through the years his operatives installed secret video cameras in all the major research centers in the United States: Baltimore, Atlanta, Cambridge and Berkley and a few lesser-known centers in New Orleans and San Antonio. His surveillance network also covered research centers in England, Germany and Sweden. And he was proud of the fact that his men had bugged the Office of the Surgeon General of the United States.

He had spent some three hundred million dollars searching for a scientific breakthrough that might save his life. Yet he had experienced nothing but disappointment until he heard the news from New Orleans.

He had ordered D'Angelo and the recovery team to go to New Orleans, grab V. J. Casstevens and bring him back to Chicago for debriefing. He had also ordered them not to harm any of the workers at the Center. However, when Star Gazer briefed him on the killings, he said nothing.

Harmon "Bruiser" Brown, one of his aides, rapped on the door. "Mr. C, Frankie is on the line from New Orleans." Harmon had served Culverwell for seven years and accompanied him everywhere he went as both valet and bodyguard. He was six-foot, eight-inches tall and weighed three hundred pounds. He played nose guard for the Chicago Bears for ten years before he retired and joined Culverwell Enterprises.

Culverwell struggled to breathe. "This is C, go a-head, Frankie."

"Mr. C., we missed the doctor."

"Yes, Star Gazer told me, and I don't like bad news."

"We're combing the streets of New Orleans and bringing in several more of our operatives to help us look for him. We just added two New Orleans police detectives on our payroll and they give me hourly re-ports on the investigation."

"Good, Frankie, find that man and bring him here."

He handed the phone to Bruiser Brown, coughed and then adjusted the oxygen tubes in his nose.

"Mr. C, will you retire for the night?"

"No man, we're right on the threshold of victory. That scientist down in New Orleans may have found the cure for the worst disease in the world. And every-body thought he was such a fool. No, I'll not sleep, call Jill and tell her to get the Surgeon General for me."

The valet dialed Jill Pettingill's room.

"This is Jill."

"Mr. C wants to speak to the Surgeon General."

"Sure, give me a couple of minutes."

When she reached the office of Surgeon General Harrison Chamberlain, she buzzed the penthouse. "The Surgeon General is on the line."

"Harrison, this is Alexander Culverwell and I want to brief you on what we believe to be a significant new development down in New Orleans." He explained in detail what his operatives had learned about V. J.'s work, his disappearance and the search for him.

"I just received a preliminary report from the New Orleans PD and they tell me we lost a number of people in the Research Center, some kind of terrorist raid. And apparently one of our scientists is missing."

"Yes, his name is Casstevens."

"We'll have operators standing by twenty-four and seven in case we hear from Casstevens and I'll ask Judd Carmichael at FBI to give us twenty agents to help us find him. Our jets will be on stand-by to pick him up when we hear from them."

"That's good and I hope he calls."

"He'll call. He has nowhere else to go."

"Yes, that's true and, by the way, I have a check for you."

"Thank you, Mr. Culverwell, it's a pleasure working with you."

"It's far more than pleasure, it's life and death, my life, my death."

"Yes, Mr. Culverwell"

"And Harrison, I have a video on the way from New Orleans and I want you to come to Chicago tomorrow and look at it with me. I believe it will be of great interest to you."

The next morning the Surgeon General arrived in

Chicago by government jet and went immediately to the Culverwell Building.

Bruiser Brown ushered him into the penthouse communications center where Culverwell was waiting. "Welcome, General Chamberlain, you are prompt and I like that."

"I always want to be of service to my friends."

The old man motioned for Bruiser Brown to play the video. "All night long I have been going over this film and find it fascinating. You know, I always believed it was only a matter of time before some scientist, perhaps in England or Germany, or in our own country, discovered the remedy for the curse of growing old. Now I believe your man in New Orleans has found that remedy and this film seems quite conclusive on the matter."

"With all due respect, Mr. Culverwell, how do you know this?"

"Harrison, as you are well aware, we have hidden video cameras in all of your research centers that are engaged in life extension research and I pay you well for the privilege."

"Yes, I am aware of that."

"Now there are two films I want to show you from New Orleans."

Bruiser Brown inserted the first video into the VCR and soon there was a clear picture of a man performing various experiments in a laboratory.

Culverwell coughed and gasped for air. "This is the lab at your New Orleans Center and the gentleman performing the experiments is Dr. V. J. Casstevens. Now look very closely."

The Surgeon General saw the man presumed to be Casstevens perform his experiment, leave the lab and go to his office where he opened a cage and released a chimpanzee. Then he saw the man inject something into the chimpanzee's left arm.

"All right, Mr. Culverwell, this is well and good, but a rather routine procedure when working with lab animals."

"Now we will look at the second film."

Bruiser Brown removed the first film and inserted the second.

"Watch very carefully, Harrison."

Chamberlain watched the man as he approached the cage and released the chimpanzee and saw that the animal looked different.

"See, Harrison, the chimp now looks younger, much stronger and energetic."

"No doubt it is a different chimpanzee."

"Not so, our cameras monitored the chimp's cage around the clock and no one went near that cage but the janitors who fed the lab animals each morning and evening and cleaned out their cages."

"Are you sure?"

"Positively. This is the same animal that was in the cage when Dr. Casstevens left the Center and, during the time he was away, the chimp made a remarkable transformation."

The film also documented V. J.'s reaction when he saw the younger chimp.

Culverwell looked up at Chamberlain from the wheelchair. "He believed someone had taken the older chimp away and placed a younger one in the cage."

Chamberlain broke out in a sweat. "I'll have to tell the president about this when I return to Washington."

Bruiser Brown ushered him out of the penthouse to the elevator where his aides were waiting. Then they returned to Washington.

Culverwell breathed hard, gasping for oxygen, then coughed and could hear the death rattle in his lungs as he told Bruiser Brown to get D'Angelo for him.

"It's ringing, Mr. C."

"This is D'Angelo."

"Star Gazer tells me we've failed again. You kill all the people in the Center and miss the one man who may have made the greatest scientific discovery in history. Dr. Casstevens is still a free man."

"Well, Boss, some of the women went nuts and started screaming and I thought the mission was in jeopardy, that's why they all had to be taken out. And I believe it is only a matter of time before we find the subject."

"I hope you are right."

Surgeon General Chamberlain stayed in his office all night hoping he would hear from Casstevens.

At seven a.m. the next morning, his secretary buzzed his office. "Dr. Chamberlain, it's the President."

He picked up the phone. "Good morning, Mr. President."

"Harrison, my sources tell me there's something big stirring at NIH. Want to brief me on it?"

"Yes, Sir, it appears one of our research scientists may have given us a breakthrough on age reversal, nothing conclusive you understand. There is some evidence that his experiments with chimpanzees have shown dramatic results. But our scientist has disappeared, vanished."

"Harrison, I've heard your boy down there is about half nuts but you know they are the ones who make all the big discoveries. And you are telling me that he may have found a way to turn back old age?"

"We don't know the full details and will have to wait until we talk to our man before we can make that determination. But it shows some promise."

"Well, keep me informed and let me know what you need."

"Director Carmichael at the FBI is sending twenty agents to New Orleans to assist the local police in their search for the doctor."

"By the way, Harrison, what about all those people who were killed in New Orleans? Did it have anything to do with the disappearance of this guy Casstevens?"

"Mr. President, we are waiting for a report from the local police investigators and the FBI down there. Right now it appears the incidents were not related," the General replied, without a hint of deception in his voice.

"Well, you're doing a good job, Harrison, and the thought that one of our men may have discovered the secret to a longer life is staggering."

"Yes, Mr. President."

Culverwell listened with great interest to the President's conversation with Chamberlain. A year earlier, completely unknown to the General, his operatives had placed listening interceptor devices on all the lines going in and out of his office. They also bugged the Centers for Disease Control in Atlanta.

He maneuvered his wheelchair across the living room of his penthouse followed by Bruiser Brown pushing a cart with two large oxygen tanks attached to his breathing apparatus. Bruiser opened the sliding doors and guided the wheelchair out onto the veranda on the fiftieth floor of the Culverwell Building.

They could see the beautiful Chicago skyline, the traffic moving swiftly along Lake Shore Drive and the lights of a dozen sailboats on Lake Michigan.

Culverwell knew the doctors were right when they said he was dying. His heart was weak and his lungs survived only a day at a time with life-sustaining oxygen pumped into his system through tanks and tubes. Although he was only sixty-two, his personal physicians told him he had worn out all of his vital organs and had the body of a ninety-year-old.

But Culverwell had never been a man who gave up without a fight. And he vowed to fight the stranger called death until he breathed his last breath.

CHAPTER NINE

V. J. didn't sleep during the night and at dawn he was still pacing back and forth in the room trying to decide what to do.

About noon, Macee opened her eyes from a deep sleep and saw Rufus lying next to her.

She kicked him off the bed. "Phew, Rufus, get out of here. V. J., can't you give this chimp a bath and dust him with some powder or something and dust yourself, too. This room stinks and I can't stand to stay in here another minute with the two of you."

"Settle down, we can't go out 'till this evening, it's too dangerous."

"So what are we going to do, *mon cherie*?"

"I guess the only thing we can do is call Washington and ask them to bring us in."

"When you talk to them tell them you don't know anything about any of this and be sure and tell them your girlfriend Macee Marineaux knows even less than you do about it.

"Why do you keep saying you're my girlfriend? We hang out together, that's all."

"Well, you'll never find any other girlfriend, the way you smell and you acting so mean."

"Hush, I've got to think. Who was responsible for all the people getting killed at the Center? Why was my office the only one that was trashed? They must have found out about Rufus and the experiment."

"Please call somebody. I don't want you to get in trouble and I'm tired and hungry and want to go home."

"Okay, settle down, I'll call Washington."

After dark they climbed down the hotel fire escape and hurried toward Chartres Street close to the Research Center and found a semi-secluded telephone booth near a dark alley.

"You got a quarter?" V. J. asked, as he looked all around for any strangers paying attention to them.

Macee handed him the coin. "You never have anything."

He dropped the quarter in the slot. "Operator, this is a collect call, person to person, to Doctor Harrison Chamberlain in Washington, D.C. at area code 202 555-1750. And this is V. J. Casstevens calling."

Janey Delaney, an FBI agent who was monitoring all the calls into the Surgeon General's office, took the call. "Office of the Surgeon General."

"This is V. J. Casstevens in New Orleans and I would like to speak to the Surgeon General."

"Dr. Casstevens, the General has been waiting to hear from you, please stand by." She alerted a tracer team that notified the New Orleans Police Department the subject was on the line.

"Dr. Casstevens, this is Harrison Chamberlain and you've had us all worried."

"Well, not nearly as worried as I am. I'm scared and in trouble and want you to bring me in."

"We already have a team in New Orleans ready to assist you. What do you suggest?"

V. J. carefully weighed the question and wondered if he could trust anyone, including the Surgeon General. "Tell them to go to the old Jackson Brewery Building on

Decatur Street in the French Quarter tonight and I'll meet them at exactly 11 p.m. A jazz group will be playing out in front. Tell your agent to give the trumpet player ten dollars and ask him to play 'Blueberry Hill'."

"All right, our men will be there. Sorry about your friends who were killed."

V. J. did not respond.

"There is talk that you may have made a marvelous breakthrough for us."

"Maybe, maybe not, but it's already cost the lives of a lot of innocent people."

Macee jabbed him in the ribs and pointed to her watch, the signal to hang up to avoid a trace. "Thank you, Dr. Chamberlain, I'll be looking for your men."

Macee looked at her watch. "Whew, that was close, seven seconds to trace."

"Okay, let's get back to the room."

Culverwell listened to the conversation from the bug in the Surgeon General's office. Then he excitedly called D'Angelo and told him of the forthcoming meeting in the French Quarter between V. J. and the FBI agents. "Don't try to take him away from the agents there in the Quarter, too many people. Follow them, eliminate the agents, and make your move."

"Yes sir, Mr, C."

After they returned to their room at the Prince Conti, Macee slept, V. J. again paced back and forth in the room worrying about the meeting with the FBI agents and Rufus drank a beer.

When Macee woke up, she stretched long and hard and rubbed her eyes. "I'm hungry."

"Yeah, me too."

V. J. looked at his watch and noticed it was nearly 10 p.m. "Hey, we've got to go. I want to get to the old brewery a little early and take a look around."

"While you do your cloak and dagger thing, I'm going to get me some *boudin*. You want some?"

"No, you know I don't eat *boudin*, can't even stand to smell the pork snouts and onions and red peppers stuffed in hog guts. No *boudin* for me."

"Well, I like it."

"Okay, go get you some *boudin* but don't draw a lot of attention to yourself. Whoever is after me must know that you and I hang out together so they'll be looking for you, too."

"Why'd you have to go and say that? I don't want anyone looking for me. I haven't done anything since I kicked that cop who gave me a ticket down in Golden Meadow and that was a year ago."

"Listen, they won't hurt you, they would probably just grab you and try to get you to tell them where I am."

"I don't want to be grabbed by anybody. I just want this all to be over."

"Yeah, me too."

V. J. took Rufus by the hand and crawled out the window, followed by Macee. They climbed down the fire escape and walked briskly through the crowded streets toward the old Brewery on Decatur Street.

"Macee, the band always sets up between Toulouse and St. Peter. I'll meet you there."

"Okay and if I don't ever see you again, it's been nice knowin' you and *Dieu vous garde*."

"Yeah, and God keep you, too. We're going to be okay." He watched her as she turned and disappeared into a crowd of people.

At 11 p.m., a large black man with dark glasses wearing jeans, a knit shirt and sneakers, eased up to the band and handed the trumpet player a ten-dollar bill and asked him to play "Blueberry Hill." The band began to play and V. J. looked all around for signs of anyone who looked suspicious.

Macee returned with her *boudin* as the band continued to play "Blueberry Hill." When they finished the number, V. J. signaled to Macee to follow him as he held Rufus by the hand and walked toward the big agent.

"I'm Casstevens."

"Good to see you, Doctor, I'm Hayes Barclay, FBI. I have a car waiting."

Agent Barclay was a classic tough guy with a gentle smile. He had a face the color of coffee grounds, with weathered crow's feet around his flinty brown eyes and V. J. thought he was the spitting image of Jimi Hendrix, the rock and roll icon of the sixties, except for one thing. He was about twice as big. *This guy really looks like Godzilla's brother.*

The agent led them across Decatur Street to an alley off of Toulouse to a white van and opened the door. "Dr. Casstevens, this is my partner, Clint Ritchie."

Ritchie nodded. "Glad to meet you, Doctor."

"Thank you and this is my friend Macee Marineaux and the chimp is Rufus."

Macee smiled. "*Enchantez*, pleased to meet you."

"And I guess in all this cloak and dagger stuff I need to ask for your ID," V. J. said.

Both agents showed him their badges, driver's licenses and FBI identification cards.

"Okay, looks good."

"We were told you would be alone," Ritchie said as

they drove out of the Quarter and headed toward the Mississippi River Bridge.

"Well, you know there are all kinds of surprises in life. Where we headed?"

"Barataria," the big agent replied.

They drove out of the Quarter to the Mississippi River Bridge and headed toward Jean Lafitte Park in Barataria.

Culverwell's operatives, who had observed the meeting with the agents, followed the van from a safe distance.

V. J. slumped down in the seat and tried to relax but his mind was spinning out of control. The two agents seemed like nice enough guys but he didn't know for sure they were FBI. *What if they are working for some rogue outfit like the one that hit the Center?*

"You guys hungry?" Agent Barclay asked. "We could stop and pick up some Po-Boys."

"That would be good and be sure to get one for Rufus," V. J. replied.

"What he needs is a good bath," the big agent said, holding his nose.

"And *mon ami*, get us some R. C. Colas," Macee added.

"There's a truck stop up ahead," Agent Ritchie said.

When they reached the truck stop, Ritchie circled the place three times, to determine if they were being followed, but never detected D'Angelo and his men. He stopped in the parking area and parked next to a giant Peterbilt truck.

"I'll go alone," Agent Ritchie said. "Be right back."

He returned a few minutes later with the Po-Boys and sodas and they sped away. The tightrope of tension they had been walking seemed to loosen up a bit as they ate.

Maybe these guys are all right, after all, V. J. decided.

CHAPTER TEN

Barataria is a hot, sticky swampland where insects, like a dark curtain, appear with the fall of night and waves of fog skim over swampy sinkholes.

V. J. had visited the area several times and was acquainted with the area. He knew it encompasses a primeval expanse of shallow pools, sloughs and Cypress swamps, and a wilderness of mists and mysteries, once the hiding place for pirates like the legendary Jean La-Fitte.

LaFitte, whose life is veiled in swampland mythology, was one of a thousand pirates who roamed the Gulf Coast in the early 1800s and robbed Spanish galleons, then sailed back into the moody, mysterious swamps with the heavy dark air, living symbols of the South Louisiana bayou country.

V. J. also knew Barataria to be the home of fun-loving Cajuns. They are French-speaking people who first migrated to the Louisiana Purchase lands from Canada in 1754.

"They chose to live in the dark, shadowy bayous and travel down hidden trails shaded by huge oaks and carpeted with Southern Shield Fern and Spanish moss hanging down like mysterious gray ghosts," he explained to Macee.

She moved closer to V. J. "I'm scared of any kind of ghosts."

The air was sweet and exciting as Agent Ritchie

turned off the highway and drove down a narrow road past fallen moss-draped trees toward the shallow back-water area marked by small, meandering sloughs.

When they reached the end of the narrow road, the big agent said, "We'll go the rest of the way on foot."

The agents unloaded their gear that included back packs, mag lights and rifles, and motioned to V. J. and Macee to follow them as they walked along a quiet path that wound its way through the oak woodlands.

V. J. looked at the open marsh and saw the freshwa-ter grasses, sedges and aquatic plants and thought the area looked like a giant arboretum. He heard the rust-ling of leaves caused by the fleeting Ground Skunks and Nine-Banded Armadillos, foraging for food on the hardwood forest floor with its tangled Cypress roots in the untamed wilderness.

The trail led into a marsh where Rufus ran after an armadillo swatting at him with his hands. But when the armadillo showed his sharp teeth, Rufus screamed and ran back to V. J. and hugged him around his leg.

V. J. smiled. "You little coward."

After they passed the marsh, the trail led into an open area.

Macee grabbed V. J.'s arm. "Look, there's a house-boat!"

"Yeah, it's a big one."

"It's no mansion but we'll make do," the big agent said.

"Well, anyway, the market for mansions is pretty well shot nowadays," Macee said. "What with the ser-vant problem and those heating bills. Besides, you can never find the bathroom."

V. J. just shook his head at her simple but honest ob-servation.

"Your home away from home," agent Ritchie said as he led them up the catwalk.

The houseboat was fifty-two-feet long, silver and blue, with a sundeck above and two decks below. There were double berths in each cabin, a large galley and a hatchway that led to the engine room where the generator, that powered the lights, was located.

Agent Ritchie cranked the motor as the big agent raised anchor and loosed the moorings. Slowly at first, the big boat cruised slowly down into the fabled bayous.

"Come on, I'll show you the galley and the sleeping quarters," the big agent said as he opened a door and went to the deck below. "You and your girlfriend can bunk here."

"She's not my girlfriend.

"Whatever," the big agent said with a wide grin on his face.

"What about Rufus?" V. J. asked.

"We'll spread a pallet on the floor and he can sleep in here with you and your friend, if you can stand the smell."

"What are we going to do for food out here?" Macee asked.

"There's plenty of food in the galley, enough to last a week."

"Are we going to be out here a week?" V. J. asked.

"I don't know, maybe longer. But at least you are safe here in the swamps, it's a good place to hide."

"Why are we hiding?"

"Dr. Casstevens, Clint and I were not given a lot of details, but apparently you are a really hot property and there are people looking for you and some of them are very unsavory characters. I have orders to keep you safe until Washington decides what to do with you."

"Do I have anything to say about it?"

"No."

The agent disappeared up the stairs to the deck.

"V. J. why did you say I'm not your girlfriend?"

"Because you're not."

"But we hang out together and have for two years and that makes us something."

"Just friends."

The next morning, V. J. went to the top deck at the very moment when night ends and the new day begins as the boat trolled through the Spanish moss and bayou mists that hide the moon. He wanted to watch the skies change colors with the new dawn and the sun come up through the towering Cypress trees with their big limbs covered with Spanish moss. A few minutes later, Macee joined him, rubbing her eyes.

"You know, Macee, the sun rises and sets in all the colors taken from the sky, the earth, the sand and sea and at the moment the sun touches them with its glowing warmth, nature has performed one of its most daring miracles, and I love it."

"You're so poetic. Did you just make up all those words?"

"No, I read them in a book. Did you sleep good last night?"

"Yeah, except for Rufus tossing and turning and wiggling. How about you?"

"Couldn't sleep, too much on my mind."

Agent Ritchie called to V. J. and Macee from the galley. "Breakfast, get it while it's hot!"

He had prepared orange juice, scrambled eggs, biscuits with sausage gravy and coffee. V. J. drank only a cup of coffee but Macee and Rufus ate two helpings of everything.

After breakfast, they went back up on deck where they remained most of the morning as the boat trolled slowly through the inland waterways, past an old Indian mound and ancient shell middens where the Indians buried their refuse. They also passed a cemetery and a Cajun fishing camp where they saw pirogues, little swamp boats, filled with handmade shrimp baskets.

They heard the raucous sounds of *zydeco* music, with its wistful, mysterious melodies, off in the distance and fits of cursing. They waved at the Cajun children jumping off Cypress limbs into the water, enjoying the pleasures of the bayou.

The houseboat moved slowly through the dark waters. V.J. saw the wind create little dust devils on a dirt road running adjacent to the bayou built by logging crews, a road with deep ruts.

Later he found several fishing poles in a storeroom and decided to try to catch some fish but gave up after about an hour. "If the fish are biting, they're biting each other."

The boat trolled past black willow, shagbark hickory and horse chestnut trees towering over Blue Flag and Wild Columbine flowers.

V. J. was enchanted by the swamps. *These people learn to survive in the rugged swamps and live in harmony with the bayous.*

The slow drift of the boat gave them time to watch the beautiful blue jays and woodpeckers and the little critters like fox squirrels and armadillos. Macee spotted two pileated woodpeckers, a Barred Owl and a Red-shouldered Hawk in the Cypress trees and a Yellow-throated Warbler nesting in the Spanish moss.

V. J. thought the quiet reverie of the swamp seemed

a long way and a lot different from the real world with its intrigue and mystery and the death of his coworkers at the Center. Deep down in his heart he wished he could stay in Barataria forever. He really liked the swamps, the scents and smells, and being face to face with another world, a safe world.

The boat rounded a bend. "Look, Macee, there's a trapper's cabin. And those are muskrat and river otter hides drying in the sun."

"Where did you learn all this stuff about the swamps?"

"Just read a couple of books. You know the swamps are a magnet for creeping things and night creatures, like sorcerers hiding behind ancient mists and you need to tune your ears to the language of the forest."

"I'd like to have a cabin out here – it's the most beautiful place on earth," she said as they passed a sunken swamp boat with the hull sticking up out of the water.

"Yeah, I guess it's okay except for the snakes, stinging insects and poison sumac. And some of the swamp people say on certain nights you can hear the laughter of the pirate Jean Lafitte echoing through the marshlands as the furies hit the earth."

"Don't talk like that, you know I'm scared of ghosts and bugs and things like that."

He laughed.

The boat passed a trapper's cabin and V. J. saw pale smoke rising from the chimney and barefoot children who waved at them from the bank.

Macee waved back at them.

Although V. J enjoyed the wonders of the bayous, he wanted desperately to make some rhyme or reason out of the horrific events of the past two days. At times self-doubt consumed him.

Did I really discover anything of scientific value? Is this sudden change in Rufus real or imaginary? Dear God, what have I done and where will it lead me? I'm not the only scientist in this land searching for the Fountain of Youth and most of the others have credentials far superior to my own. But if by some strange twist of fate I have found the secret of aging, what must I do?

V. J. felt a strange premonition that he might be probing into an area that should be left alone or just trusted to God.

But is it wrong to reach for the golden rings? It has always been a far-away dream but am I on the verge of finding the pathway that would allow us to live a hundred fifty or two hundred years and be vigorous and in good health all throughout that extended lifespan?

The question tormented him.

He could see a remarkable transformation in Rufus but he didn't know if humans would experience the same dramatic change.

And even if it works with humans, how would we ever be able to come to terms with the ethical considerations of who should receive the treatment and who would be denied?

Macee held his hand in hers as the sun cast long shadows through the swamps. "Look, there goes the sun, everyday it goes and someone always goes with it."

She is so free. Maybe I should be more like her. But she can sure be dingy at times.

He remembered the day he asked her date of birth.

"July fifteenth."

"What year?"

"Every year."

V. J. smiled and shook his head.

Suddenly Macee broke the quiet reverie of the bayou and began to dance all around the deck singing, "Ladies and gentlemen, hoboes and tramps, cross-eyed mosquitoes and bow-legged ants."

"Macee, where did you hear that song?"

"Never heard it, just made it up. You like it?"

"Yeah, I like it."

"Want to hear it again?"

"No, once will be enough."

"V. J., what's so bad about feeling good?"

"Well, put a few brain cells into action and see what you come up with."

"Chill out, you're going to give me a bad case of the hives. You know what, you need to clean up, dress up, shape up and quit worrying so much."

V. J.'s face turned red. "Listen, nearly all the people in my office have been killed, some bad guys are looking for me, I don't know what to do and you're giving me all this personal advice."

Her countenance dropped and he noticed a sad look on her face.

V. J. felt a tinge of guilt for his sour attitude toward her and knew the mess they were in was not her fault. And he realized she just wanted to help.

But she has never heard the job of Saviour has already been taken. Sometimes she acts like God has left town and put her in charge.

"*Mon cherie*, do you have to pay dues to be a Catholic?" Macee asked, changing the subject.

"I thought you were Catholic."

"No, not since I was a little girl down in Golden Meadow, but I ought to be something because any worldly experience is a universal kind of thing."

"So what are you trying to say?"

"Oh, I don't know." She smiled and blew him a kiss.

"Do you know what today is?"

"No, and please don't keep me in suspense."

"Today is the tomorrow we worried about yesterday, and everything turned out all right."

Macee stopped talking and appeared to be in deep thought.

It troubled V. J. for she seldom was quiet. "What are you doing?"

"I'm thinking."

"Well, the first time is always the worst."

"Don't make fun of me, I'm not an airhead and I'm educated far beyond my years. Why don't you just tattoo 'dummy' on my forehead, maybe that'll be kicks."

"Aren't we touchy?"

"Well, you make me mad always puttin' me down."

"You know I don't mean anything by it."

"How's a girl to know?"

V. J. knew that Macee had a pure heart and if God ever sent down a thunderbolt it would probably miss her and hit him.

And, she did save me from those two big guys in the Quarter, whoever they were.

Macee settled down. "V. J., you really need to smile more because did you know that every seven minutes of every day someone in an aerobics class pulls a hamstring?"

"Two things, I don't know and I don't care."

"Sure, you've had some bad things laid on your table, but it wasn't my fault so don't take it out on me. And besides, on everybody's calendar there are some rainy days."

V. J. knew she was right, but wondered what mysterious hand of fate led this woman into his life.

"Guess what, V. J., the other day I was at the supermarket and this old lady swung her purse at the grocer for taking out his dentures and wiping them with his red handkerchief while she was in a hurry to get her onions weighed."

"Why don't you just sit and be quiet for a few minutes, all your talkin' and wigglin' around tires me out. Besides, I need to sort out some things, my research, the killings, lots of things."

She decided to try to cheer him up. "Well, I want to talk. Did I ever tell you about Great Grandpa Jules Marineaux who was a Rebel soldier in the Civil War?"

"No, I can't recall that you ever told me that story."

"Well, Great Grandpa Jules was a rebel fighting for the South at Shiloh and got shot in the eye by a musket ball. The doctors patched up his eye but never did find that musket ball."

"So what happened to him?"

"Well, if you'll give me time, I'm getting to that. Some forty years later he was sittin' on the front porch of his home down in Golden Meadow and was dippin' W. E. Garrett Snuff and spittin' in a tin cup."

"Yeah and..."

"He was dippin' and spittin' and all of a sudden he sneezed real hard and that musket ball popped right out of his nose and landed in that tin cup and just rolled around."

Oh Lord, please give me a burst of patience.

A few minutes later, Macee handed him a birthday card with a picture of her on the front, a card she made herself at Wal-Mart.

He opened the card and read a note. "Dear V. J., birthdays are good for you because the more you have the longer you live. Love, Macee."

"This is real nice, but how did you know it was my

birthday?"

"It's on your driver's license."

"Yeah, okay."

They stood there side by side in the hypnotic silence saying nothing as night fell and the boat drifted through the bayou darkness on its way down to the sea.

CHAPTER ELEVEN

The idea of calling Luka Avanzini, the son of New York City crime boss Rocko "Big Daddy" Avanzini, left a bad taste in Wu-tang Fong's mouth. Why should I risk blowing my cover by consorting with known members of an organized crime family? He wondered.

Wu-tang Fong picked up the phone and dialed Luka Avanzini's home.

A maid answered. "The Avanzini residence."

"This is Wu-tang Fong in Chinatown and I would like to speak to Mr. Luka Avanzini."

"Mr. Avanzini is not available at the present time."

"Please tell him this is a matter of grave concern and could be quite rewarding financially for him."

"Please hold."

A few minutes later a voice on the phone said, "This is Luka."

"Mr. Avanzini, this is Wu-tang Fong of the House of Fong Imports and Exports."

"Yeah, that nickel and dime stuff, I've heard of you on the piers. Some of my boys roughed up a couple of your chinks and it was all over nothin', a measly two grand a week in protection."

"Mr. Avanzini, I would like to meet with you on an important matter if you would be so kind as to join me in the banquet room of the Forbidden City Restaurant on Forty-Second Street at 8 p.m. this evening."

"Naw, we're not interested in imports and exports

and I don't know what you could talk about that would be of interest to me."

"I'll assure you it is of the utmost importance to you and your father, Rocko Avanzini."

"So, how's that?"

"I read in the *Daily Express* that he is ill and failing more every day. What if I were to tell you there may be some hope for your father?"

"Some chink acupuncture cure?"

"Not at all."

"We've had the best doctors money can buy and got nothing."

"What if there was a new method of treatment, with miraculous curative powers, that only a few people know anything about? That would certainly be worth exploring, I believe."

Luka said nothing as Wu-tang Fong waited impatiently.

"Yeah, maybe so, tonight at eight at the Forbidden City, but you better not try to snake me."

"Yes, I understand."

The long, black limousine stopped in front of the Forbidden City Restaurant and three of Luka Avanzini's bodyguards jumped out and checked the street. One of the men opened the door for Luka and the four of them entered the restaurant.

The head waiter bowed and greeted them. "Welcome, Mr. Avanzini. Your host is waiting for you. Please follow me." He escorted them toward the back of the restaurant and opened the door to the banquet room where a dinner had been prepared for them.

Wu-tang Fong met them at the door and bowed. "It is a great honor to meet you, Mr. Luka Avanzini."

Luka shook hands with Wu-tang Fong as his men

looked all around the room and checked the side rooms and windows.

"Thank you for granting me the honor of this meeting. I am your humble servant and I believe our meeting will be mutually beneficial."

"Yeah, what you got?"

"Mr. Avanzini, you and I are both businessmen. You undoubtedly have roots in Sicily as I have roots in China, the land of my ancestors."

"Well, I ain't got much for Sicily no more. I'm a New York City kind of guy."

"Yes, and I have chosen New York City to be my home. But I have friends and relatives in my mother country and from time to time I am able to assist them in small ways."

"Okay, Mr. Fong, tell me what you got."

"My homeland needs your help."

"Ain't nothing I can do for China."

"Perhaps there is."

"I'm listening."

"Mr. Avanzini, what if I told you there is a scientist who has found a way to reverse the process of growing old?"

"Say what?"

"I mean making old people young again."

Angered, Luka stood, snapped his finger and motioned for his men to get ready to leave. "Mr. Fong, you bring me downtown and lay a fairy tale on me and waste my time, don't ever do that again! I'm Luka Avanzini!"

"Please hear me out. My country has scientists who are engaged in research in Russia, the United States, Germany and Japan."

"Yeah?"

"One of our scientists in Moscow is doing research on the problems of aging. He says the entire scientific world is buzzing with a report out of New Orleans that a scientist there may have discovered a way to make an old person much younger."

"Don't try to con me, man, I ain't no scientist but I know when you're old you're just old and ain't nothing you can do about it."

"But what if there is something in science that you have never heard of and know nothing about? And what if there is some new discovery that could heal your aging father of his infirmities and make him healthy and vigorous again?"

"You're serious, aren't you?"

"Yes, and the Chinese government wants to retain you to find that scientist and bring him back to New York City where I will arrange for him to be sent to China?"

"What's in it for me?"

"Ten-million dollars up front and, as soon as we learn the specifics of this new scientific discovery, ten million more and your father will be among the first to receive the new treatment."

"The Avanzini family is not into kidnapping. That's a bad rap and the feds never give up 'till they find you and put you away for a long time."

"Perhaps you should discuss this matter with your honorable father, Rocko Avanzini."

"I speak for the family! But yeah, I will mention it to the old man."

Wu-tang Fong smiled and bowed to Luka Avanzini. *This young punk is insolent and arrogant and doing business with him makes me sick.*

After dinner, Luka snapped his finger and motioned

for his bodyguards to check the hallways. "I'll contact you in a couple of days."

"Thank you, Mr. Avanzini."

Wu-tang Fong escorted the party out the side door of the restaurant to their waiting limousine and spit in their direction as they sped away.

CHAPTER TWELVE

V. J. and Macee sat down at the table in the galley and watched the Evening News on an old black-and-white television set.

The top story was a follow-up on the killings at the center.

"The search continues for Dr. V. J. Casstevens, the only survivor of the massacre at the National Research Center earlier this week," the anchorman said. "Weegie Peabody, secretary to the director, died this morning at LSU Hospital from complications after her fall from a second-story window during the mass murders. She was the only survivor."

"Macee, Weegie died!"

"Yeah, that leaves only you."

After a commercial, the report continued. "Now we go live to the downtown Police Headquarters where our Hilary St. Clair is standing by with Detective Lieutenant Scott Dula, who is leading the investigation into the killings."

"Thank you, Lieutenant, for speaking with us. Is there anything new that you can tell us about the killings at the Research Center?"

"Not much at this time but we believe the raid on the Center had something to do with Dr. Victor Casstevens' research and what he may have discovered. And I would like to urge the doctor, if he is watching this newscast, to come on in and let us protect him from those men who killed his coworkers."

"Since Dr. Casstevens is the only survivor, does that make him a suspect in the murders?"

"No, we do not think that he was implicated in any way. But I do believe his life may be in danger and I would strongly urge him to let us bring him in."

"Thank you, Lieutenant Dula, until the next time, and again, anyone who knows the whereabouts of Dr. V. J. Casstevens should call Lieutenant Scott Dula at the Downtown Police Station," she said as the station flashed a picture of V. J. on the screen.

"Thank you," Dula replied.

"This is Hilary St. Claire, Channel 26 News."

The anchorman also reported that Arthur "Jango" Terhune, a noted New Orleans jazz pianist, had died and a jazz funeral was planned for the next day in the Quarter.

V. J. shook his head. "Too bad about Jango. He was one of the great ones."

"Yeah, I liked him, too. Do you want to play some pinochle?"

"Yeah, why not?"

However, when she melded the queen of spades and the jack of diamonds scoring forty points, it made V. J. so mad he threw his cards on the table and went to the refrigerator to get him and Rufus a beer.

Macee glared at him. "Boy, are you uptight, or what?"

The big agent was standing guard at the keel, chewing on a cigar and listening to the frogs, crickets and other sounds of the night creatures in the swamp.

Agent Ritchie went to the other side of the boat to relieve himself when a man in a dark rubber wet suit reached up out of the murky water, grabbed him by the legs and pulled him off the side of the boat. Then he plunged a knife into the agent's stomach just below the ribs, killing him instantly.

A second man, also wearing a dark wet suit, slowly made his way through the shadows onto the deck of the boat behind the big agent. He slipped a piano wire around his neck to garrote him but the big agent thrashed and jerked and both of them fell into the water where the intruder tightened the piano wire crushing the big agent's esophagus.

V. J. heard the splash in the water and rushed up on deck to look around. He saw the agent and the man in the wet suit thrashing around in the water.

He ran back down to the galley. "Macee, we've got to get off this boat, now!"

"Why, what –"

"Don't ask, Macee, just do as I tell you!"

Fear paralyzed her as she ran up to the deck.

V.J. squeezed her hand. "Now jump."

He picked up Rufus and threw him screaming into the murky bayou waters and took a last look across the deck before he jumped into the water beside Macee.

The water felt tepid and heavy as they swam away from the boat toward a shadowy canopy of moss-draped Cypress trees. V. J. knew that some foul stroke of evil had befallen the agents and was sure he and Macee were in danger from some unknown enemy.

After they swam through the waterways for an hour, Macee motioned to V. J. "I'm tired and can't swim anymore. And besides that, I've got to pee."

"Just dog paddle and try to hold it for a while."

"I can't hold it, I've got to stop and pee."

"We can't stop, it's too dangerous."

"Well, I'm tired and wet and scared and I'm not going to pee in the water."

"Okay, let's head for the bank."

He swam to the bank, grabbed some vines, pulled himself up out of the water and reached down to help Macee and Rufus, who snorted then dashed into the woods.

Macee walked over behind a large Cypress tree, dropped her cutoffs and relieved herself.

She returned and sat down at the base of a large oak tree beside V. J. "I guess you know this has been the worst night of my life. We're out her in the middle of a swamp with gators and cottonmouth moccasins and lizards and I don't like it at all."

She began to cry and V. J. put his arm around her and drew her close to him.

"It's okay, we're going to make it out of here."

"Somebody up there better mark this down for me," she said, pointing toward heaven. "V.J., you scared?"

"No, I always turn this shade of yellow when the sun goes down," he replied as a shooting star lit up the purple sky.

She snuggled up real close to him and realized this was the second time he had hugged her that day.

"What you doing hugging me? You said I'm not your girlfriend."

"Maybe it's because our bodyguards just disappeared, we're lost in a swamp and there may be some really bad dudes out here looking for us, that's why."

"I thought maybe it was because you had started liking me."

She walked around to the other side of the tree, stripped down naked then squeezed and twisted the water out of her cutoffs and put them back on.

V. J. was tired and wanted to sleep but he knew

sleep would not come easy. "We'll hang out here until daylight then try to find our way back to the fishing village."

"How far is it?"

"I don't know, maybe five or six miles."

"Well since we're out here in the jungle all alone, what would it take for a girl to get a kiss?"

"Chloroform."

"Where's Rufus?"

He was chasing and pawing at a nutria. The little furry creature snapped at him. He screamed and climbed a tree where he rested on a limb.

V. J. had a bad taste in his mouth as the events of the past few days turned sour on his stomach. *Who would want to take Macee and me away from the FBI agent? Was it the CIA? Maybe the devils that killed the people at the Center. Were they government agents gone bad or a freelance outfit that found out about my work? But how would they know where we were? I told no one but the Surgeon General. This is like the vivid nightmare of a frightened sleepwalker.*

V. J. looked up into the starry sky. "Lord, you haven't heard from me lately, but how can I make amends for all the things I've done if you don't pull us through this mess?"

Tears tricked down Macee's face and she wiped her nose with her arm. "You know Hayes and Ritchie were my friends."

"You only knew them for a couple of days."

"But they were nice to me and I liked them."

V. J. knew they were in danger and the men responsible for the disappearance of the agents would have search teams all over the swamps looking for them. He guessed they would bring in dogs and helicopters to join in the search.

"We'll rest here for an hour and then double back to the village and try to rent a boat and make our way to the ranger station at Jean Lafitte."

"I'm hungry and a big mosquito just bit me right on my butt and it itches," Macee blurted out shattering the stillness of the dark swamp night.

"Well scratch it."

"You scratch it for me."

"I'm not going to scratch a mosquito bite on your butt."

"And I'm scared, what if I get bit by a water moccasin?"

"The snake is probably going to be more scared of you than you are of it."

"If he is then he's shakin' real bad all over," she said, her voice scratchy and dry, her dark eyes dancing.

"We'll find a way out of here."

"Well, if I die I'm going to call you on the phone and say, 'This is Macee Marineaux calling from the grave, wish you were here.'"

"You're not going to die."

She decided to change the subject. "You know how you can tell a real Cajun from everyone else?"

"No, but I'm sure you're going to explain it to me."

"They know which leaves to use for toilet paper."

She laughed as she picked up some leaves and walked behind a large sycamore tree.

V. J. sat down flat on the leaf-covered forest floor and listened to the wind blowing in the tops of the oak and Cypress trees. A few minutes later Macee returned and sat down beside him.

After they rested for an hour, V. J. looked up through a canopy of trees and watched the coming of dawn as the sky softened a bit around the edges. He could see that it was pale and pink even though he only saw soft patches through the giant trees. Time seemed to stand still until sometime later when the sunlight just jumped up and started dancing in the wind and he could hear the soothing whispers of the wind in the leaves.

He shook Macee to wake her and they set out for the fishing village through the swampy marshland where the vegetation was so thick they could see only a few feet in front of them. As they made their way through the unfriendly woods, V. J. dodged swampy sinkholes and smelled a hint of rot in the thick muggy air as his lungs pumped hard for oxygen.

They were wet with sweat as they walked slowly through the hostile woods and moved from sunspots to tree shadows. V. J. saw a faint trail that sneaked off into the thick woods with tangled vines and interlocking trees on either side. "Come on, Macee, let's follow this trail."

He noticed pussy willows were beginning to bud beside puddles of clear water as they walked on a carpet of fallen leaves through which a tiny strawberry plant and a wild violet, putting forth tiny white blossoms, were growing.

Every few steps V. J. reached back and tugged at the seat of his britches.

"Your underwear ridin' up on you?" Macee asked.

"No, now hush and come on," he said as they walked across a grassy flat toward a grove of trees. "This sure isn't like the Barataria travel poster."

"Can we stop for a few minutes, V. J., I got a stomach ache."

"It's just gas, now come on, we've got to find that fishing camp."

"It's not gas because I haven't had anything to eat and I can't go any further."

"Yes, you can."

CHAPTER THIRTEEN

Culverwell took a deep breath of oxygen, wheezed, coughed and wiped the sweat off his forehead with a damp towel.

"Get Frankie for me," he told Bruiser Brown.

"Yes Sir."

Minutes later Brown said, "Mr. C., Frankie is on the line."

"Hello, Frankie, what you got down there?"

"We neutralized the two FBI agents on the riverboat but Dr. Casstevens and the broad are slippery and they got away."

"Frankie, I pay you two hundred grand a year for this bad news? What are you and the boys doing, standing around pulling hairs out of your butts?"

"We have ten men searching the swamps now and twenty more on their way down here from New Orleans. We'll cover all the trails in and out of here."

"I hope so, Frankie, and when you do, take good care of him. He may be the most important man in this land, maybe in the whole world. And get him back to Chicago immediately. Do what you want to with the girl."

"We'll find him, Mr. C, and I have a Lear standing by in New Orleans to transport him to Chicago."

"That's good, Frankie."

When Harrison Chamberlain arrived back at his office he was mobbed by reporters who had heard rumors of a major scientific breakthrough in New Orleans that may have been related to the deaths at the National Research Center.

Chamberlain had already been on the phone at his home for an hour with Clark Cameron of the *New York Morning News* who was doing a story on the New Orleans killings. Cameron asked all kinds of questions about the Center's research in age reversal and life extension and Chamberlain wondered how he learned about the research. He could tell from the nature of the questions that someone had leaked at least part of the story and it troubled him.

"Dr. Chamberlain, the AP is reporting a major scientific advance in your Research Center in New Orleans. Could you tell us more about it and is it related to the murder of your top scientists in that city?" Pete Caldwell of the Western Broadcasting Company asked.

"I have no comment except to say that the unfortunate deaths of our people in New Orleans are still under investigation."

"Doctor, there are reports that one of your scientists who survived the attack on the Center is missing, could you comment on him and his whereabouts?" Matthew Markham of the Associated Press asked.

"We have FBI agents in New Orleans assisting the Police Department and they are conducting a thorough investigation."

"Can you confirm that you have a scientist who is missing?" Markham asked.

"We will have a report for you as soon as the investigation is completed. Thank you, ladies and gentlemen," Chamberlain said as he walked through the host of reporters to the front door of the NIH Building and on to the elevator.

When he arrived at his office, his secretary said, "Mr. Chamberlain, the President is on the line."

"Thank you."

"Yes, Mr. President."

"Harrison, we're going to have hell to pay with the American people if you fail to clean up this mess in New Orleans. My Secret Service boys have just informed me there is a free lance group down there looking for Dr. Casstevens."

"A free lance group?"

"Yes, some players we know nothing about, probably the ones who hit the Center. And Walker at Justice says the FBI has lost two agents down there, hasn't heard from them since yesterday. These were the men we sent to bring in your man."

"You mean they are missing? And what about Dr. Casstevens?"

"Walker isn't sure. And Harrison, we're getting calls from Japan, Germany, Brazil and they all want to know if we've discovered the Fountain of Youth. Have we found it?"

"Mr. President, I honestly don't know. We'll just have to wait until we find Casstevens and check out his research."

"And we better find out about the rogue operation in New Orleans. Someone may have lowered the standard for paid killers."

"Yes, Mr. President."

CHAPTER FOURTEEN

Several Culverwell search helicopters cross-crossed the Barataria swamplands. V. J. and Macee hid under the heavy foliage until the copters passed then continued through the swampy marshlands toward the Cajun village, careful to make a wide circle around the area where they believed the houseboat was located. Rufus jumped from tree to tree and swung on vines.

Macee looked through a canopy of trees at the aircraft flying at treetop level. "Those helicopters make me nervous. They're looking for us, aren't they?"

"Yeah, but it's okay, they can't see us in these heavy woods."

"Well, I sure hope not."

They walked down worn pathways and deer trails through the hypnotic silence in a land where there was nothing time had not touched.

Macee saw a red fox with his head cocked and his tail curled over his toes, a heavy-furred animal that showed no fear of the intruders in the forest.

The wind whistled through the trees and except for an occasional panther scream deep in the bayou the only other sound was the gentle whisper of falling leaves and the occasional rat-tat-tat of the helicopters.

They walked several miles and V. J. thought he heard voices.

He grabbed Macee's arm. "I believe this is the fishing camp but we must make sure the people are friendly."

Streaks of blue smoke rose from the house and hovered over the surface of the swamp. V. J. smelled the scent of burning tobacco from the camp, a smell that carried far into the woods.

He watched the village for nearly an hour to make sure it was safe. "Okay, Macee, let's do it."

"*Bon jour* the camp!" Macee called out. "*Ici on parle Francais?*"

A small woman with dark eyes and careless hair stepped through the pale smoke of the campfire. "*Bon jour,*" she said with a soft, seductive voice and a Cajun accent.

"My name is Macee Marineaux and this is V. J. Casstevens."

"*Enchantez.*"

V. J. noticed she had older eyes in a younger woman's face, eyes darker than wine.

Macee spoke to the woman in French and learned her name was Princess LaCaze and her husband Henry was the head of the camp. For the next ten minutes the two women engaged in an unquenchable stream of bright, wild talk.

The camp house was made of hand-hewn Cypress timbers, with pegged attics and rock chimneys. V. J. noticed there was an outhouse, hen house and doghouse.

"V. J., Princess tells me her husband is fishing off of Grand Terre, a barrier island, but will be home later this afternoon. And she said two men came to the camp earlier today and asked if she had seen any strangers."

Princess LaCaze invited V. J. and Macee into the house and served them thick black coffee. Her husband Henry returned about mid-afternoon and Princess introduced him to V. J. and Macee. V. J. looked at him and thought he was hot-wired by too many years of evolution. He wore a heavy beard and had a slight whistle when he talked. Looking at him caused V. J. to realize that man is a creature wrapped in mystery.

"They must go to Jean Lafitte and want you to take them there," Princess told her husband.

LaCaze agreed to take them by boat to the ranger station at Jean Lafitte but, after hearing that the two men had been looking for strangers, said they should travel at night. Then he picked up a jug of moonshine, removed the cork and pulled hard twice, then offered the jug to V. J who shook his head.

"Does he know the swamps well enough to travel by night without lights?" V. J. asked Princess.

"Yes, he grew up in these swamps."

V. J. and Macee slept the rest of the day. After dark, LaCaze woke them and motioned for them to follow him around to the back of the log house to a slip where his flat-bottom boat was tied off.

"*Merci boucoup,*" Macee said to Princess LaCaze with a smile.

"*Soyez le bienvenue,*" Princess replied.

After they stepped down into the boat, LaCaze jerked the starter cord one time and the motor cranked. Then they moved slowly into the dark waterway.

As the burly fisherman skillfully maneuvered the boat through the shallows, he blew his nose and a bug came on his handkerchief. He looked surprised as he wiped it off on his pants.

They passed two small islands and an old Indian burial and ceremonial mound, and V. J. thought the slow drift of the boat through the moss-draped Cypress trees was very peaceful. For a moment he forgot all the trouble he faced back in New Orleans.

They arrived at the Park and LaCaze pointed to a light in the distance and, in broken English, told Macee it was the Ranger Station. Macee reached over and hugged their Cajun guide. "*Merci boucoup*, Mr. LaCaze."

"*Dieu vous garde*, may God keep you."

LaCaze disappeared into the swamps as they headed for the light they believed to be the Ranger Station.

They approached the station house and V. J. heard voices. He grabbed Macee's arm and put his fingers up to his lips. "You wait here, I'll take a look."

"Don't leave me out here alone. You'll come back, won't you?"

"Yes, I'll come back."

V. J. moved closer to the house and saw two men dressed in black carrying automatic weapons standing near the front porch. His gut feeling told him they were looking for him and Macee so he quietly backed away and returned to where she was waiting.

"We've got to get away from here, far away." He led her down one of the nature trails in the park, hoping it would take them to the entrance.

After walking for several miles, V. J. saw headlights from a car and guessed they had found Highway 31, one of the main routes to the Park.

They walked another two miles down the highway, hiding in the shadows when cars passed by, to a truck stop with dozens of big rigs parked in front.

"Macee, I'm going inside to call Washington. You stand watch and if you see somebody who looks suspicious, come and warn me."

"I don't want to wait out here."

"It's okay, I'll be right back."

No one paid any attention to him as he entered the

large building where there was a restaurant, convenience store and bunks and showers for the truckers.

He spotted a phone in the hall outside the showers
and dialed the Surgeon General.

"This is the Surgeon General's Office, how may I
help you?"

"I'm V. J. Casstevens and I need to speak to the
man."

"Yes Sir, Dr. Casstevens, please stand by."

Seconds seemed like hours as V. J. waited for his
boss to answer the phone.

"This is Harrison Chamberlain and I've been expecting your call."

"All hell's broken loose down here. The two agents
you sent to bring me in are dead and I'm wondering
who's killing who."

"Doctor, we believe there is a rogue unit in the New
Orleans area, mercenary types sent there to kidnap you,
the primary reason being you may have made a heretofore unthinkable scientific discovery during your experiments on the chimpanzee."

"We'll talk about that later, right now I just want
you to bring me in."

Then he wondered how the Surgeon General knew
about Rufus. *I have never mentioned that the experiment
was done on a chimp. Perhaps he knows more about this than
he leads me to believe.*

"There may be some people who are in a big hurry
to find you and are willing to take the necessary risks,"
Chamberlain explained.

"Is that why I'm running?"

"Yes, but on the matter at hand, we still want to
bring you in."

"What you got in mind?"

"A CIA unit has been dispatched to New Orleans to pick you up. Of course they are working closely with the FBI."

"Yeah, and everybody I know in the FBI is dead."

"That's unfortunate. We now believe it would be in everyone's best interest to get you out of New Orleans so that we can take certain precautions. Now where are you, Doctor?"

"You know, the last time you asked me that question I told you but it got me in a lot of trouble and some guys tried to kidnap me." V. J. was aware that an honest enemy is far better than a dishonest friend. And he wondered about Chamberlain. "I'm running out of reasons to trust you. This time we'll do it my way."

"Of course."

"There is going to be a jazz funeral in the French Quarter tomorrow afternoon. The procession will march down Esplanade."

"Yes, Doctor."

"There will probably be a pair of matching gray horses pulling the caisson behind the jazz band and when they reach Rampart Street, have your man walk beside the caisson for one block. Then, tell him to light a cigar and keep walking with the mourners until I contact him."

"Alright, Doctor, three CIA men will be there to pick you up and get you out of there."

"Thank you, Dr. Chamberlain."

V. J. and Macee hitched a ride back to New Orleans in a big rig leaving the truck stop. When they arrived, they went immediately to the Quarter and rented another room at the Prince Conti for the night.

Culverwell personally monitored the telephone conversation between V. J. and the Surgeon General. "Good, that's good!" Then he told Bruiser Brown to get D'Angelo for him again.

"Yes Sir, Mr. C.," Frankie D'Angelo said.

"We are going to have another shot at Casstevens."

"That's good news."

Culverwell explained how V. J. would make contact with one of the CIA agents. "They are sending three agents to New Orleans to pick up the doctor and our contact at CIA says that one of them, an agent named Morgan, has done some work for us before. Perhaps you should contact him as soon as he arrives down there and explain the situation to him."

CHAPTER FIFTEEN

The next morning V. J, Macee and the chimp walked across the Quarter to Rampart Street and climbed up the stairs to the roof of an apartment building where they would have a clear view of the jazz funeral as it approached from Esplanade. V. J. knew they would also be able to spot the CIA agent with the cigar.

The jazz players, accompanied by a twenty-four voice black choir from Memphis, approached their position. V. J. saw a man walking alongside the caisson light a cigar.

"Come on, Macee, we're going to follow the parade for a while."

"I'd rather watch it from up here where I can see everything."

"Just come on," he said, pulling on her arm and leading her down a flight of stairs to the street below as Rufus tagged along.

They followed the procession for several blocks, pushing their way through the throngs of people lining the streets.

"Macee, I want you to do me a favor."

"What do you want now? I've been stuck off in that stupid swamp and have mosquito bites all over my butt and I'm tired."

"Contact the agent smoking the cigar."

"No, not this time."

"Please, you just tell him that Dr. Casstevens sent

you and I'll be on the lookout to make sure no one has followed him. Then you can bring him into the alley at the next intersection."

"Well, if somebody has followed him that means they will get me and not you."

"Trust me."

"Yeah, I trusted you and it nearly got me killed twice."

"Just do it."

"Okay, but if they get me it's going to be all your fault."

"They're not going to get you."

"Would it be possible for a girl to get a kiss in case I never see you again?"

"You don't need a kiss and you are going to see me again."

"Not even a peck?"

"Maybe a peck." He reached over and kissed her on the forehead. "Now go on, Macee."

"That was nice."

Macee followed the agent who was walking beside the caisson. After a couple of blocks, she walked up behind him and tapped him on the shoulder. "Dr. Casstevens sent me."

"Where is he?"

"He's going to meet us in the alley off of the next intersection."

"Okay, let's go."

The agent followed Macee down the street, through the crowds of people, to an alley where V. J. was waiting.

"Dr. Casstevens?" the agent asked.

"Yes, I'm V. J. Casstevens."

"Good, I'm Max Thurman, CIA, let's get out of

here."

They walked several blocks to where the agent's Ford Explorer was parked. He unlocked the door on the passenger side and motioned for them to get in. Then he drove several blocks to the ramp that led up to Interstate 10 and headed north toward New Orleans International Airport at Harahan.

The agent entered the airport and drove to a row of private hangars, pulled up in front of Hangar Number 3 and stopped. Two men opened the sliding door and the agent drove inside where V. J. saw a sleek blue and white Lear Jet.

Agent Thurman slid out of the Explorer and went around to the passenger side and opened the door. "Okay, here we are."

The agent introduced the other men. "Doctor, this is Mike Morgan, our pilot, one of the best in the Agency. And this is Jack 'Pig Iron' McDaniel, another one of our agents."

V. J. shook hands with both of the men. "Would it be presumptuous to ask where we are going?"

Thurman nodded. "Not at all. We're going to Arizona where we have a safe house near Superstition Mountain."

"Never heard of it."

He introduced Macee, who was holding Rufus by the hand, to the agents and after a couple of minutes she reached over and whispered, "I've got to use the bathroom."

"I saw a toilet up by the entrance, and take Rufus."

"Take him yourself, I'm not going to let him watch me use the bathroom."

"Heaven's sake, he's a chimpanzee."

"I don't care."

About 4 p.m., Lieutenant Dula and Detective Francis were returning to the Police Station from their follow-up investigation at the Research Center when they received a radio message from Central Dispatch. "Car thirty three, what's your location?"

"We're ten-two-five your twenty, ETA about five minutes," Dula replied.

"Well, the Chief just got a call from the park ranger down in Jean Lafitte in Barataria. The ranger says a couple of FBI agents had a houseboat in the bayou and brought along a couple of guests to do some fishing."

"Okay, what else?"

"This morning the ranger was cruising the bayous and found the boat but the agents and their guests have disappeared. The Chief wants you and Charlie to go down there and see what's going on and find out if there is some connection with the killings at the Research Center."

"Ten-four, we're on our way."

The Lieutenant turned on the flashing lights and raced across the Mississippi River Bridge and on toward Jean Lafitte State Park.

The park ranger met them at the main entrance.

"Hello, I'm Antoine. Thanks for coming down. I don't know exactly what we have but it looks suspicious."

"I'm Scott Dula and this is Charlie Francis."

"Okay, gentlemen, we're going for a ride." The ranger led them down a narrow path into the swamps to a flat-bottom boat.

He pulled the cord and the motor started and they sped through the bayous and backwaters for about twenty minutes. When they rounded a bend, Dula saw the large houseboat drifting with the fog under the heavy Cypress shadows.

The ranger pulled up close and motioned for the detectives to go on board.

They climbed up the side to the sun deck as the boat gently swayed back and forth in the water.

Dula went down the stairs to the galley where he saw a deck of playing cards, a glass of iced tea and a couple of empty beer cans on the table. But there were no signs of foul play.

"Whoever was here left in a hurry," Francis said. "They took off without their duffel bags and clothes."

"But why would somebody jump ship out here in the middle of a swamp?" Dula asked.

"There may be some kind of swamp monster out here," Francis said, trying to add a little levity to the situation.

But Dula didn't think it was funny and glared at him. "Charlie, go ahead and get our people down here, and ask them to call in a fire rescue team to drag the bayou. I don't like this at all."

"Scott, I've found something!"

"What you got?"

"This cigar – it burned out on deck, like someone dropped it."

"Yeah, you're right."

Francis keyed his radio. "Car 33 to Central."

"Central, go ahead Car 33."

"We are down in Barataria and Lieutenant Dula wants a forensic team down here ASAP and send a fire rescue team. He wants to drag the bayou."

"Ten-four, Car 33."

"And Charlie, you will be our contact man with the feds. Try to find out what their agents were doing down here and if anyone has heard from them."

"This bayou won't give up its secrets," the ranger said. "At night the gators come out and if there were any bodies in the bayou there would be no trace after the gators finish with them."

Dula frowned, a look of exasperation on his face. "You mean, no bones or nothing?"

"That's right, the gators catch their prey and drag them into small caves and under ledges in the bayou. Your divers won't find anything but maybe a belt buckle or a pair of shoes."

The forensic team arrived and Dula and Francis returned to the city.

Late that afternoon Chief Landry summoned Dula, Francis and Jewel Fontnote to his office to bring him up to date on the investigation of the mass killings at the Research Center.

Dula and Francis arrived and greeted Jewel Fontnote who was visiting with the Chief's secretary.

The secretary greeted the detectives. "Good morning, Scott, Charlie, the Chief will see you momentarily."

"Yeah, whatever," Dula said.

A few minutes later Chief Landry opened his door. "Alright, come on in and let's get started."

They entered the office where the walls were covered with awards and citations the Chief had received during his forty years on the force.

Dula shook hands with the Chief who was tall and lean and looked much younger than his sixty years. From his rookie days, Dula had heard of the legendary exploits of Chief John David Landry, a no-nonsense, untouchable kind of guy who had survived years of graft and corruption in the New Orleans Police Department and emerged as clean as a hound's tooth.

Chief Landry lit a cigar. "Okay, what you got?"

"A dead end," Dula replied. "Except for one thing, I received a call the other night from Dr. Casstevens. He told me he was the one who called in and reported the killings."

"Does it look like he could be involved?"

"Chief, right now we can't even place him at the scene of the crime."

"You mean he wasn't there?"

"Said he wasn't."

"What do we know about his work at the Center?"

"I called NIH in Atlanta and they say Casstevens is quite a remarkable character," Francis replied. "He was engaged in some kind of research to find a way to help people live longer lives."

"Like how long?"

"Maybe a hundred fifty, two hundred years."

"Is this supposed to be reliable scientific research?"

"The people in Atlanta told me there are research centers all over the world trying to find out what makes people grow old and how to do something about it."

A wide grin creased the Chief's somber face. "I'll tell you exactly what makes people grow old, it's being a cop in New Orleans."

He pulled off his glasses and rubbed his bushy eyebrows. "Well, the department is in a lot of hot water over these killings and some heads could roll. I want to know every detail and each new wrinkle in the case. Anything else?"

"Well, Chief, it may be nothing, but my people picked up a partial print at the Center, the only one we found as the intruders undoubtedly wore gloves but one of the guys apparently snagged his glove on a broken piece of glass for that's where we picked up the print," Jewel Fontnote said. "We sent it to the FBI lab and they got back with us and said the print belongs to one Healy John Cathcart of Chicago."

"What else?"

"The bureau said years ago Cathcart did a nickel in Joliet for running a protection racket on the Chicago south side but their records show he has been clean for several years. He lives with his wife and two children in a high-dollar high-rise up on State Street in Chicago, according to the IRS, and works for a company by the name of Tower Leasing, Inc., a subsidiary of Culverwell Enterprises, Inc. of Chicago."

The Chief scratched his head. "What would a dude from Chicago be doing in New Orleans? And what about Culverwell Enterprises?"

"Culverwell is a giant real estate holding company owned by Alexander Culverwell who is reputed to be one of the richest men in Chicago and something of a recluse. That's all the info the bureau had on him."

"He's never been tied to organized crime or anything like that."

"No, nothing."

"Okay, Scott, I want you and Charlie on the next plane to Chicago and set up a surveillance unit on this Healy John Cathcart and find out what his fingerprint is doing in the Research Center in New Orleans. And keep in touch with me every few hours because the mayor and the city council are going crazy over this thing. I'll contact Chief Mike Murphy in Chicago and ask him to get some of his CID boys to give you a hand."

"If something develops, we'll let you know," Dula said as the Chief stood, shook hands with each of them and escorted them to the door.

CHAPTER SIXTEEN

Agent Morgan, the CIA pilot, asked V. J. and Macee to board the plane then he taxied onto the tarmac. A few minutes later the tower instructed him to take off from Runway Nine. Soon they were airborne.

"If you're hungry, there's plenty of food in the galley," Agent Thurman said as he unbuckled his seat belt, stood and stretched.

"Yeah, I'm hungry," Macee said. "I'll fix some sandwiches. Got any sodas?"

"In the refrigerator."

Morgan climbed to thirty thousand feet, put the Lear on automatic pilot and joined the others in the cabin.

"Doctor, now we can brief you on what's going down," Thurman said.

"Well, go ahead."

"As you know, the FBI lost two agents in the Barataria swamps but, of course, you and your girlfriend miraculously escaped."

"She's not my girlfriend."

"Well, whatever, the President asked the agency to help out and our boss Hank Browne at CIA sent us to bring you in. We'll keep you and your friend at a safe house near Phoenix at a place called Superstition Mountain until things cool down some and then move you on to D.C."

"Yeah, we believe you'll be safe," Agent McDaniel

added.

"Safe from whom?"

"Doctor, there are a lot of people looking for you, both inside and outside the government," Thurman said. "You're about the hottest property in the country. And, tell me, Doctor, is it true? Did you discover some kind of pill that will stop old age?"

"Mr. Thurman, I'm not really sure what I have discovered. I was conducting lab tests on a chimp when everything went sour and people started getting killed."

"Well if you have found a way to slow down getting old, my hat's off to you."

"Yeah Doc, got any samples?" "Pig Iron" Jones asked.

"I've only tested one chimpanzee."

"Yeah, in one week Rufus went from being an old chimp to a much younger one after you gave him the shot and is getting a little younger every day," Macee said.

"I need a lab for further testing to see if I can repeat the process with other animals. Then, based on those tests, I would try it on humans."

"You can test me," Thurman said. "I've got twenty-five years with the agency and plan to retire next year. I wouldn't mind going back to eighteen or nineteen again."

"Pig Iron" Jones laughed.

"NIH is sending several trucks with a complete laboratory to Arizona along with lab animals and everything else you will need," Thurman said. "It will be set up in a prefab building adjacent to the safe house."

"We need to call the agency and let them inform the SG that we've brought you in and everything is okay,"

"Pig Iron" Jones said.

Jones dialed the agency in Washington and asked to speak to the director.

"Stand by, Agent Jones," the secretary said.

"This is Browne, I've been waiting for your call. And you have some good news?"

"Yes, Sir, we brought in Dr. Casstevens, his girlfriend and the chimp you told us about."

"Where are you now?"

"We're on our way to Superstition Mountain to the safe house."

"Good show, agent Jones, I'm proud of you guys. Our trucks with the lab and the animals will be on the way to Arizona tomorrow morning."

V. J. was sitting by the window on the right side of the cabin but as he looked out into the starry sky he could not find the North Star.

He glanced over at the pilot. "That's interesting. If we're headed west why can't I see the North Star?"

"Maybe it's just hazy."

"No the night is clear."

"Well, I don't know. The compass is pointing west."

V. J. asked agent Jones if he could borrow his phone and dialed the Surgeon General's Office.

"This is Chamberlain."

"V. J. Casstevens. The CIA agents picked us up and we're on our way to Arizona."

"I'm glad you're finally safe."

"Yes, that makes two of us."

"Director Browne tells me the agents who brought you in are the most trusted men in the agency. I know you've been through a lot but now you're safe and as soon as the field lab arrives, you can continue your research."

"Thank you, Sir, I appreciate the field lab."

"And if you need anything else, give me a call. By the way, Doctor, the President is very interested in the work you are doing."

"I'm honored, Sir, and I'll go to work as soon as the lab arrives. But you understand it will be necessary for me to conduct dozens of tests on the animals before I test any humans."

"Yes, I understand. There's no hurry."

"Thank you, Sir."

"Goodbye, Dr. Casstevens."

"Goodbye, Sir."

Culverwell, who had monitored the entire conversation, whispered through a malignant smile, "You're wrong, Dr. Chamberlain, dead wrong. I'm in a big hurry."

CHAPTER SEVENTEEN

The phone rang at 2 a.m. and startled Wu-tang Fong out of a deep sleep. He threw the covers back and reached for the receiver. "Wu-tang Fong speaking."

"Yeah, Fong, Luka Avanzini."

"Yes, Mr. Avanzini."

"My old man and I want to meet with you tomorrow morning at our place on Long Island around ten. Can you be here?"

"Yes, Mr. Avanzini, at ten."

"Okay, my boys will be looking for you."

Unable to sleep, Wu-tang Fong went to the kitchen and brewed a pot of coffee.

So this lowlife decided to help us. Maybe it's the twenty million. Or could it be his old man? Whatever, I'll be glad when I no longer have to deal with street trash like Luka Avanzini and his father.

Wu-tang Fong drove away from the city, through the tollgate near Long Beach to the Robert Moses Causeway that would take him to Babylon and the home of the Avanzinis. Rain squalls appeared out over the ocean with a colorful rainbow in the east then floated away.

He approached the Avanzini estate surrounded by high walls with a bright blue gate. A guard stopped him, ordered him out of his Mercedes and frisked him.

"The Avanzinis are expecting you. Follow the road and you'll see the mansion just around the first curve."

"Yes, thank you."

He drove along the road with manicured lawns and hedges and beautiful rose gardens on both sides and saw teams of armed men with Doberman Pinscher guard dogs walking along the inner perimeter of the mansion grounds. He waved to the guards who just stared at him. The mansion grew larger and more beautiful as he drew closer. It was a magnificent old colonial mansion, framed by tulip poplars and facing out over the ocean. Olive trees flanked the entrance on either side. *I guess this gives these spaghetti benders a touch of Italy.*

Wu-tang Fong saw cool gray and green flower beds filled with lilies, Lemon-Gem Marigolds and feathery yellow-headed dill in front of the house and a few raspberry brambles scattered around the garden. He walked up to the mansion past a Victorian-style urn filled with Aloe vera and blades of ivy foliage at the base and an American flag furled in the wind on a pole beside the urn.

The butler opened the door. "Welcome to the home of the Avanzinis."

"I am Wu-tang Fong of the House of Fong."

"Yes, the Avanzinis are expecting you."

He followed the butler down a long hallway where he saw a prayer altar with an open Bible in front of a beautiful candelabra. They entered a large drawing room with walls lined with bookcases with all the works of Shakespeare, books by Tom Clancy, John Grisham and F. Scott Fitzgerald, and a complete set of the Statutes of Law of the State of New York. A large picture of Rocko Avanzini, over the mantle of the fireplace, dominated the room.

This is the classic picture of capitalistic excess, Wu-tang Fong thought as he looked around the room at the pieces of Sheraton and Chippendale, Waterford glass and Chinese porcelain. *At least they have the good sense to display our porcelain.*

Crime really pays and pays big, he thought, as he listened to the voice of the far-famed Italian tenor Enrico Caruso singing *Ole Sole Mio*, coming into the room through two large speakers near the door.

A few minutes later the door opened and Luka Avanzini and his father Rocko Avanzini, confined to a wheel chair, entered the room. Luka moved his father up to the table. "Fong, this is my father Rocko Avanzini."

Wu-tang Fong reached out toward the old man to shake his hand but he did not respond. "It's my honor to meet the great and renowned Mr. Rocko Avanzini."

The old man nodded.

Wu-tang Fong noticed a caste of death on the old man's face as he sat with his head bowed, his hands folded. *He's just about gone and I'm sure this world would be better off without him. But not before we entice his son into helping us find Dr. Casstevens.*

"My father does not speak but he writes a few things down on paper and he wants to hear more about the doctor you mentioned to me."

"Yes, the doctor, of course."

Rocko Avanzini raised up in the wheel chair and looked at Wu-tang Fong through troubled eyes.

"The scientist in question is Dr. V. J. Casstevens of New Orleans and there are those in the world's scientific community who believe he has made a major breakthrough in the understanding of the process of aging and how to reverse it. However, the doctor disappeared from New Orleans a few days ago and has not been heard from since."

"How do you know that he has made such a discovery?"

"Although I am an American citizen, I have many contacts in Beijing from where I import most of my wares. Beijing has scientists studying in all the major centers of the world and they affirm that the word out of Washington is that Dr. Casstevens has in fact made such a discovery."

"Now Fong, we have contacts in New Orleans, as a matter of fact I go down there several times a year to check on some of our financial interests and to visit with the governor. And I've done a couple of favors for a police captain down there. He may be able to help us."

Wu-tang Fong thought Luka Avanzini was a boor and quite annoying but he also knew that he was the man for the job and that pleased him.

"Then you are interested in doing business?"

"Yeah, for the twenty million. That's chicken feed, change, we make that in a week, sometimes more. But we'll take the risk if you can help my old man. But he wants some kind of assurance that he will be the first to get the treatment from Dr. Casstevens.

"It will be a bargain if you can find Casstevens," Wu-tang Fong said. "Now I wish to call our embassy in Washington."

"Yeah, use this phone."

Wu-tang Fong reached the Chinese ambassador and informed him that the Avanzinis had accepted the proposal. They spoke animatedly in Chinese for several minutes on another matter. Luka Avanzini and his father Rocko didn't understand a word.

He hung up the phone. "The ambassador is quite

pleased and he said that once Dr. Casstevens is appre-
hended, he will be placed on a ship bound for China
and you and your father will be welcome aboard the
ship for the treatment you expect your father to receive."

A slight smile creased Rocko Avanzini's lips and he
nodded ever so slightly showing his approval.

"When will we get the twenty mil?" Luka Avanzini
asked.

"It will arrive in the city by courier in three or four
days, and I will personally call you when we have it in
hand. You can pick it up at the House of Fong after you
deliver Dr. Casstevens."

"Okay, we'll let you know when we have the doctor."

Wu-tang Fong bowed to the Avanzinis and Luka escorted him to his car and watched him drive away.

Luka Avanzini spent the rest of the day calling in his
top men from Detroit, Los Angeles, Cleveland and
Miami. He told them something big was going down
and he wanted them in New York the next morning.

He also called Police Capt. George Blaine in New
Orleans, an officer who once was a target of the local
mob until Luka intervened on his behalf and saved his
life.

"Captain, this is Luka Avanzini."

"Good morning, Mr. Avanzini, it's been a long time."

"Yes, but you know we are friends and sometimes
friends go to one another for help."

"Yeah, that's the way it works."

"Now, Captain, I need your help."

"How can I help?"

"There is a scientist by the name of V. J. Casstevens
missing from the Research Center in New Orleans and I

have been retained to find him. Can you help me?"

There was a pause on the line. "Mr. Avanzini, I think we need to continue our conversation on my cell phone. I'll call you back in about five minutes."

"I'll be waiting."

Captain Blaine went downstairs and out the front door of the station to his police car, then dialed Avanzini's number.

"Yeah, go ahead."

"Mr. Avanzini, here's the word around the station. There were several scientists killed at the National Research Center and the Chief assigned Lieutenant Scott Dula to run the investigation. At first there were no witnesses, no motive, nothing. Then they got lucky and picked up a print of this guy in Chicago who works for a man named Alexander Culverwell. And that's about all there is except Dula and his partner, Charlie Francis, are on their way to Chicago following that lead. I understand he reports to the Chief a couple of times a day."

"Captain, I'm sure you know Johnny 'The Wire' Bravo who at one time was connected to the Marcello family."

"Yes, I think he's still around."

"I want you to get in touch with him and tell him to bug the Chief's office tonight and I know you will give him whatever cover is necessary."

"Yes, Mr. Avanzini, and I will assign a man tomorrow morning to monitor the bug."

"Thank you, Captain, and I hope you will keep me informed as to any future developments. And I'll have something in the mail for you today."

"Thank you, Mr. Avanzini, it's always a pleasure doing business with you."

"Yes, and with you. I'll put in a good word with the governor in Baton Rouge on your behalf."

"Thank you, Sir."

By mid-morning all of his most trusted men had arrived at the mansion and Luka Avanzini escorted them into his personal study. There was Billy "The Foot" Frazier, an enforcer who grew up on New York's east side before Luka sent him to Detroit to take over the Avanzini family operations there. Luka also welcomed Bailey "The Bull" Buchanan, head of operations in Cleveland, Joey Falco from Los Angeles and Ramon Chavez from Miami.

Each of them knelt down and kissed Avanzini's hand and pledged their allegiance, even to the death, to the Avanzini family.

"You are the men I trust, there are no others so trusted. And you are aware that we have been very successful these many years bringing in millions from our labors and, God as my witness, I have shared liberally with you and made you wealthy men."

All the men nodded their heads in agreement.

"But you also know that my father, Rocko Avanzini, is sick unto death and even with our great fortunes, we are helpless to make him well. However, through some act of good fortune from God, there is a man who has found a way to make my father well and even take away some of his many years."

Each of the men looked at one another startled.

"Yes, it is true. The man is a scientist and he made the discovery in New Orleans a few days ago. Now our organization has been asked to find this man. Although there will be a sizeable monetary reward, the most important reward is that my father will be the first person to be treated and for that I would give up everything I own."

Tears streamed down his face as he continued to speak of his father.

"We have a lead down in Chicago and I want you all to be ready to go there on a moment's notice."

CHAPTER EIGHTEEN

Agent Morgan glanced back into the cabin several times and waited until V. J., Macee and the other agents were sound asleep. He inserted a clip in his Nine Millimeter Beretta, screwed on a silencer and put the Lear on autopilot. He walked slowly back to the cabin and fired two shots instantly killing Agent Thurman, then Jones, who stood and reeled in a bizarre dance of death before Morgan shot him a second time.

Rufus heard the muffled shots and squealed and started jumping over the rows of seats.

The noise startled Macee. When she saw the two dead men, she screamed and shook V. J. "Wake up!"

Morgan looked at her menacingly. "Okay, lady, just sit back down real easy."

"What's going down, man?" V. J. asked Morgan.

"You'll find out soon enough."

"Your friends, are they dead?"

Morgan replied with depraved indifference. "They weren't my friends. We were a team for a hundred covert operations and we killed people and blew up buildings but we never became friends."

"You murdered your own men. You can get the needle for that."

"Murder? Yeah, that's what I do for a living. But I'll dodge the needle, you'll see."

"Why did you do it?"

"An old man paid me two million cash to deliver

you to Chicago, that's why. We'll be there in about three hours."

"You sold out your friends for money?"

"Yeah, the mighty green dollar. You got to run at it to get it. The love of money is only half the root of all evil, the lack of it is the other half."

"What about us?"

"Look, Doctor, I don't care what becomes of you. I know the government is hot to bring you in and sent us down to New Orleans for that purpose. But I made a better deal."

"What happens when we get to Chicago?"

"I turn you over to the man."

"What man?"

"The man who paid me two million. Money talks, you know, and when there's lots of it, it screams."

"What's going to become of you?"

"I'll just disappear to some Polynesian island where there are beautiful women, lot's of booze and I'll live like a king and drown myself in pleasures the rest of my life. Makes me proud to be an American."

"Someday you'll be sorry for what you've done."

"Don't mess with me, Doctor, you're going to make me bust out crying. Anyway, my conscience quit me thirty years ago and I'll die with a smile on my face."

"You've sold your soul to the worst kind of devil."

Morgan glared at him.

"You can't kill two CIA agents and walk away – they'll chase you to the ends of the earth."

"If I'd wanted my fortune told, I'd called a Gypsy. One of these days you may even wish you were in my shoes."

"Right after hell freezes over."

V. J. felt like a character in a cheap novel who has a

premonition of death after the world spills over on him scalding hot. *This guy is as crazy as a man can get and still be standing. He killed his friends for a lousy two million bucks.*

Macee, still trembling, raised her hand.

"What you want?" Morgan asked.

"I've got to use the bathroom."

"Well go on, but don't take too long."

Macee walked toward the rear of the plane, stepped inside the toilet, locked the door and relieved herself. She felt safe there.

I need to do something, but what? Something, anything.

She poured all the contents of her purse out on the floor and saw a fingernail file.

Hmm, maybe, just maybe.

She raised the toilet lid and used the file to remove the screws that held it in place. Then she waited.

Morgan glanced at his watch and thought Macee had been in the toilet a long time but guessed she was just doing whatever women do in places like that. He walked to the back of the plane with his pistol in his right hand and used his left hand to turn the doorknob. Suddenly Macee shoved the door open so hard it knocked him down. He fired several wild shots as he fell. Then she hit him in the head with the toilet seat and knocked him out cold.

Rufus screamed again and jumped into the middle aisle and hid under some blankets.

"Whew, I didn't think he was ever going to open that door."

V. J. picked up the pistol and slapped the agent's face a couple of times to revive him but there was no response.

"Macee, we got trouble now. Why'd you hit him so

hard? He was our only ticket out of here."

"I didn't like him pointing that gun at me."

"I know and you did good. But I can't wake him up and I sure can't fly this plane."

Macee looked over at the window and saw it was covered with oil. "V. J., look, what's that on the window?"

V. J.'s heart jumped up and lodged in his throat. The window was covered with an oily substance and he was sure it was jet fuel. He guessed that a stray bullet from Morgan's gun punctured the fuel tank.

"Macee, come on, let's check the cockpit."

"What for?"

"I want to look at the fuel gauge."

V. J. scanned the instrument panel but could not find the fuel gauge.

"There it is," she said, pointing to the gauge.

"It's nearly empty."

"I'm scared and I'm sorry I hit him so hard."

"It's okay, honey."

"Honey? You called me honey? Does that mean that you like me?"

"Well, a little, you're okay."

V. J. rushed back to the cabin and once again tried to revive the pilot. "He's still out cold."

"What are we going to do?"

"I don't know. Perhaps one of these days we'll wake up and find this was all a bad dream."

V. J. could tell the plane was losing altitude and he guessed they had only minutes before it would crash.

"Lord, I can't think of anything Macee and I have done to deserve all this and if you have any ideas on how to get us out of here we need to hear from you real soon. And, by the way, this would make a guy want to do the promise to God thing, and I'm seriously thinking about it."

"V. J., I know how we can get out of here."

"How, Macee?"

"I saw some parachutes in the cabinet in the toilet. Maybe we could bail out."

"Macee, we don't even know where we are. We could be over water or some mountain range and could get ourselves killed."

"Well, we don't have a lot of choices. I've jumped a lot of times, nothing to it."

"What you talking about?"

"I got into sky diving right after I dropped out of college."

"You never told me."

"You never asked."

Macee found two nylon parachutes folded into cotton duck packs and brought them back to the cabin..

She strapped a chute to V. J.'s back. "Now, you fasten the pack with these harness straps."

She hurriedly buckled the straps on her pack then checked V. J.'s once again to make sure it was secure.

"You've got two lines, one to go left and the other to go right. And this is the ripcord. You hold it with your right hand. We're going out freefall and as soon as you clear the plane give it a good jerk."

"What if it doesn't open?"

"It will open, these are sport parafoils and they are a lot safer than regular chutes. They have a sleeve that draws the parachute upright and keeps is from getting tangled."

"That makes me feel a whole lot better."

Macee removed the pilot's leather belt and strapped it around Rufus's waist, then fastened it to the harness on V. J.'s chute.

"And remember, *mon cherie*, landing is like jumping off a ten-foot ladder. Keep your knees bent and hit the ground with your shoulder, then roll over to cushion the shock."

V. J. heard the engines cut out and the plane went into a dive.

Macee opened the plane's side door.

"Okay, V. J., you go first and holding your breath won't help!" she yelled over the roar of the rushing wind.

"After you."

"No, jump!"

She shoved him out the door and shouted, "Geronimo!"

The wind whistled around his ears and the cold air caused him to tremble. Rufus grunted and seemed to be enjoying the ride.

Seconds later Macee jumped out headfirst and went into freefall.

V. J. jerked the ripcord. His pack's cover flipped open, a small pilot chute popped out and soon filled with air, creating a strong upward force of drag which pulled the main chute out of the pack.

After Macee jumped, she saw the Lear crash into a forest below, but it did not explode.

Their chutes floated slowly through the cool, crisp night in the bright moonlight.

V. J. tried to remember Macee's instructions about landing. She said for him to keep his knees bent and hit the ground with his shoulder down then roll over to cushion the shock.

He landed and did exactly as Macee told him but his chute's suspension lines became entangled in some saplings and he realized his underwear had turned around bad on him.

Rufus grunted and licked him on the ear.

V. J. stood up, unbuckled the straps and looked around for Macee.

"Hey, V. J.!"

He followed Rufus as he darted through the tall grass into the nearby woods.

"Macee, where are you?"

"Over here, help me!"

V. J. moved through the moonlit darkness toward a small creek lined on either side by sycamore trees.

"Up here! My chute is caught in the tree."

"Well, what do you want me to do?"

"Climb up here and cut me loose."

"With what?"

"It would help if you had a knife."

"You know I never carry a knife. You're just going to have to stay up there until it gets light and I can figure out a way to get you down."

"Don't make me get tough with you," she said as she felt her jeans riding into the unknown. "Besides, both of us need to get a health plan and some life insurance because things are getting dangerous."

"Please, this is just not the time."

Rufus scampered up the tree and sat down on the limb by Macee.

"Well I can't spend the whole night up here."

"Then get down by yourself."

"Who was it that got us down here, anyway?"

"Macee, hush."

"I'm scared and I don't want to fall and hurt myself."

"You fell ten thousand feet already."

"Just do something, I don't like this at all."

"*C'est la vie,* that's life, as you Cajuns would say."

"Oh, you're so helpless."

"At least I'm not tangled up in a tree."

V. J. slept beside the tree until a couple of hours before daylight when Macee yelled at him. "V. J., get me down out of here!"

He rubbed his eyes and surveyed her situation. In the moonlight he could see the chute's suspension shrouds hanging precariously from the limb of the giant sycamore tree, about ten feet from the trunk and thirty feet from the ground. The lines that connect the canopy to the harness were still anchored to a ring on the harness that was wrapped around her waist.

"I'm going to walk down the creek and see if I can find some way to get you down."

"Well for heaven's sake, don't get lost and leave me stranded up here and I'll never see you the rest of my life and if I die it will be all your fault."

"You're not going to die."

V. J. walked down the creek past fallen trees with gnarled roots and as his eyes adjusted to the darkness he could see the smooth landscape with monotonous vegetation, tall grass and bushes covered with berries.

He reached some shallows where he decided to cross the creek. He looked down and saw a glint from the moonlight through the crystal-clear water. The creek bed was covered with sharp rocks.

"Okay, Macee baby, this may be your lucky day." He reached down and picked up two of the sharpest rocks he could find.

Then he returned upstream to where Macee was still dangling from the tree limb, with Rufus at her side.

Macee heard him tramping through the leaves.

"That you, V. J.?"

"Yeah, and I've got an idea."

He pulled off his shoes and looked up at Macee. "I'm going to climb the tree and cut the lines of your chute."

"Well hurry because I've been here all night and I've got to pee."

"Why didn't you go ahead and pee?"

"In this tree, thirty feet in the air? You've got to be kidding. And besides, Rufus is looking."

"Macee, Rufus won't mind."

"But I will."

V. J. climbed up the tree, reached the first limb and pulled himself up to where Macee's lines were caught. "I hope this limb is strong enough to hold us both."

He crawled toward her and removed his belt. "Here, Macee, put this belt around the limb and then around your waist. I'm going to cut these lines."

"Okay, but be careful."

V. J. removed the sharp rocks from his pocket, held one of the lines against the limb and began striking it cutting it in two. He worked feverishly cutting all the other lines and within minutes Macee was free.

He reached out and took her arm. "Now remove the belt and let's get down out of here."

"Whew, I was scared."

"Yeah, me too."

They climbed down the trunk of the tree and when they reached the ground Macee gave him a big hug and he hugged her back.

"Macee, you know you saved our lives up there, taking out Morgan and finding the chutes."

"Does that make me your girlfriend?"

"Yeah, sorta." He smiled, put his arms around her and kissed her.

Rufus was jealous. He licked his face.

Macee thought the kiss was as poignant and endur-
ing as a love poem.

At 8 a.m., Chamberlain called Culverwell and informed him the CIA plane was missing.

"Air Traffic Control in St. Louis said the plane
dropped off radar about 2 a.m. this morning. It was in a
wooded area about a hundred fifty miles northeast of
St. Louis."

"Were there any survivors?"

"We don't know but our teams are on the way to the
crash site with the investigators from the FAA to make
that determination. We should know something in a
few hours."

"Anything about Dr. Casstevens?"

"Nothing yet."

"You know, Harrison, if he dies, one of the world's
great dreams dies with him."

"Hopefully he is still alive."

The next morning when Wu-tang Fong read the
Morning News he saw a brief article about a plane crash
in Missouri, a plane believed to be carrying Dr. V. J.
Casstevens, a New Orleans scientist.

According to the article, when search teams reached
the plane they found three bodies believed to be CIA
agents, but there was no sign of the doctor or his lady
friend.

Wu-tang Fong immediately contacted the Chinese
Embassy in Washington. "There's bad news, Mr. Ambassador. Beijing must be advised that Dr. Casstevens is
missing somewhere in Missouri."

"Yes, Mr. Fong, I will relay your message to Beijing

immediately. But I suggest you contact the Avanzini family and make them aware of this most recent development."

"Yes, Mr. Ambassador."

Chapter Nineteen

The danger excited, yet unnerved V. J., and served as a constant reminder of the limitations of his life. But he was determined to survive. Although he couldn't walk on water or read the future, he gritted his teeth and said, "Macee, we're going to make it out of here and then we'll try to find a safe place to hide. I'm tired of running and being pushed around."

He motioned for her to follow him and started at a dogtrot down a narrow trail that led across a choked little stream near low ridge lines, up a knoll and across a large field with corn stalks still standing. He wanted to cover a lot of ground before daylight and find a hiding place where they could sleep during the day.

They ran through the twilight for an hour, almost ghostlike and invisible, across several gullies and grassy flats toward a grove of trees by a wide stream. A cloudy mist blanketed the sky as they came up on a heavy thicket. "This will give us some good cover where we can rest," V. J. said.

V. J.'s leg muscles ached and his stomach cramped. He slumped down in the thick grass. "I ache all over and what doesn't ache doesn't work."

"V. J., my britches are too big, they keep falling down."

"Well gain weight."

"You won't like me if I'm fat and can't climb down out of a tree."

He listened in the woods for the sounds he didn't want to hear, the brush of leaves, the cracking of a twig, a dry limb breaking underfoot, anything that would indicate they were being followed. But all he could hear was crickets and frogs.

Macee snuggled up real close to him and put her arm across his chest.

In a few minutes she was sound asleep but V. J. was restless as he tried to analyze the frightening events of the past few days. *The lust for immortality must be endemic to the human experience and somebody from Chicago paid Morgan a bundle of money to satisfy that lust. But I still have no clue as to who is looking for us, or who killed the workers at the Center or the agents who tried to help us. And it's getting a little tiring.*

After dark they followed a deer trail down to a river. They walked along the riverbed for several miles through the clear moonlit night looking for a shallow crossing to the other side.

"Macee, let's ford the river here and head west."

"Well I don't want to drown."

"You're not going to drown, now take my hand."

They walked slowly out into the water and across the river then continued on through the woods and open fields until they came to a dirt road.

"Okay, Macee, let's follow the road and see where it takes us."

"I'm tired and don't want to go any further and my feet are wet."

"Just a little further. It'll be daylight soon and we can rest."

They walked about a mile along the dirt road when V. J. saw a pale light through the woods. "There's a light."

"Yeah, wonder what it is?"

"I don't know, let's take a look."

They drew near to the light and V. J. saw a rustic old log cabin and a ramshackled clapboard barn beside a small creek with wisps of fog clinging to the water. He listened for any sounds from the house but heard none and, since there were no dogs barking, decided to hide out in the barn and try to get some sleep.

V. J. opened the barn door. The hinges squeaked and frightened Macee.

"V. J., be still, you're going to wake up the dead!"

"Hush, and come on."

He closed the door. It was dark inside the barn except for the light from the moon's yellow haze filtering through the cracks between the sideboards.

V. J. saw a small haystack at the back of the barn and motioned to Macee to follow him. "We can sleep here for awhile and hope no one finds us."

Soon both of them were sound asleep.

A couple of hours later, the squeaking door awakened V. J. He looked up he saw an old man carrying a lantern and pointing a double-barreled shotgun at them.

"Git up and explain yourself. Caught you trespassin' in my barn and I ought to shoot both of you right here and now."

V. J. raised his hands over his head. "Hold on, old timer, we don't mean you any harm. We've been lost in the woods and traveling most of the night so we decided to try to get a little rest."

"I knowed who you was soon as I seen you. The radio talked about it, the plane crash and some people missin'."

The old man motioned with the shotgun for them to

get up. "Now, no funny stuff cause we're going out in the light where I can get a better look at you."

V. J. saw his gnarled finger on the trigger of the shotgun. *I wonder why God has chosen me for this penance.*

V. J. knew one thing for sure, it wouldn't be wise to make the old man nervous.

They walked through the squeaking door into the early morning light. V. J. noticed the old man had a heavy gray beard and several layers of dark wrinkles on his face. One eye was considerably bigger than the other and V. J. couldn't tell if he was looking at him or Macee for one of his kotch eyes went off to the left, the other to the right. The years seemed to have beat the old man down real hard. He had the traces of care and sorrow on his face, a face as sad as it was angry.

"My name is V. J. Casstevens and this is Macee Marineaux. We are survivors of the plane crash trying to find our way back to some town."

"I don't care what your name is, I'm going to load you in my pickup and drive you to town and turn you over to the sheriff, maybe I'll collect a reward."

"We're not fugitives and there's no reward, we're just lost and need help."

"Where you live?"

"New Orleans."

"Hot-dog, got me a couple of good ones from New Orleans."

"Mister, what's your name?" Macee asked.

"Cole Thompson, but never mind my name, I'm taking both of you in."

"You know, Mr. Thompson, I'm kinda hungry, think you could let me stir up some breakfast before we go?"

"What you got in mind?"

"Maybe some biscuits and gravy and have you got

any side meat and a few eggs and some syrup?"

"Hmm, that sounds good, yeah, we can wait a spell while you fix some biscuits. But no funny stuff."

The one-room house was a wreck with clothes scattered all around, dirty dishes on the oak table and trash on the floor.

The old man turned to Macee. "You ever used a wood cook stove?"

"Yes, my grandmother had one down in Louisiana."

"Well, there's plenty a kindlin' in the box so go ahead and scrape us up somethin' to eat, I'm hungry, too."

Macee made the biscuits from scratch, fried the side meat and eggs, and fixed a big skillet full of flour gravy.

"Nothing wrong with a good home-cooked meal. Now I'm going to lean this gun up against the wall but don't try nothin'. I'm old but I'm still fast on my feet."

The old man ate like a field hand and only stopped occasionally to belch. When he finished, he said, "Now that was fine."

"Thank you," Macee said.

"How long you lived here in Missouri?" V. J. asked.

He wiped gravy off his beard with his shirtsleeve. "More'n twenty years, moved back here from the Bitter-roots Mountains in Montana where I was a mountain man and trapper. Yessiree, trapped beaver and hunted griz."

The old man paused, sopped his biscuit in the gravy one more time and continued his story. "Got married, lived up above the timberline for thirty years and my wife turned meaner and uglier ever day. Thirty years is a long time to fight it out with jest one woman."

"What happened to her?" Macee asked.

"One day she passed, buried her in an aspen grove

near a creek with runnin' water."

Macee smiled.

"Yeah, but now I'm full as a tick and sleepy, so I'll jes take me a swig or two of the recipe." He opened a cabinet door and took out a quart jar half full of moonshine whiskey. "Made it myself in the still back in the woods, best shine this side of St. Louie. We'll talk about going to see the sheriff a little later on."

Macee watched in amazement as he took two long pulls on the whiskey, wiped his mouth with his sleeve, then killed the rest of the bottle. "Now I'm just gonna ease back in my chair and..." he said as he folded his hands across his stomach and his words trailed off into a deep sleep.

Macee took a blanket off the bed and gently placed it over the old man to keep him warm.

V. J. signaled to Macee that it was time to go and she followed him outside into the front yard and beyond to the woods in the distance. They walked through the woods in a northerly direction most of the day and just after sundown came to a country road.

"Maybe we can hitch a ride," V. J. said as they walked along the road. After a couple of miles they saw a sign that said: "The Dutchman's Saloon, Two Miles."

They arrived at the Saloon where they saw Budweiser, Coors and Miller's signs on the front of the building and a couple dozen Harley-Davidson Motorcycles parked outside.

V. J. approached the saloon cautiously, looked through a dirty window and saw people milling around. He slowly opened the swinging doors, stepped inside and walked over to a dusty soda-pop machine.

The air smelled of smoke, beer and urine. There were at least two dozen bikers and their women drinking beer, arm wrestling, throwing darts and several were listening to cheatin' songs.

V. J. squeezed Macee's hand. "Must have been a jail-break somewhere."

A couple of the bikers had already passed out at their table but no one seemed to be paying any attention to them. Two others had the full-body dry heaves and headed for the toilet. Another staggered around like a drunk trying not to hit a telephone pole and vomited all over the floor.

An old janitor, with a crooked nose and bleary eyes, mopped up the mess and seemed relieved when the task was completed. Although some of the stench disappeared, the smell remained and it made Macee a little dizzy.

V. J. stepped up to the bar where he saw the bartender mixing tomorrow's hangover. He had a mad look on his face and was mumbling something about one of the bikers dropping a cherry bomb in the toilet.

The bartender looked at Macee. "Anymore like you at home?"

She did not answer.

"V. J., I've got to go to the ladies room."

A drunk turned to V. J. and said, "Guess what, I just saw a horror show on TV, the six o'clock news. Want to know something else? I was the electric shuffle-board champ at the McTavish Bar in East St. Louis." Then he laughed so hard he spilled his beer.

V. J. smiled but said nothing.

Macee returned to the bar. "That toilet stinks and there's a man in the women's room passed out on the toilet stool."

"Yeah, Macee."

"What will it be?" the bartender asked.

"How about a couple of cold ones for me and my friend and one for the chimp."

"We don't serve monkeys in here."

V. J. thought the bartender looked like he had once been the poster boy for Perverts R Us and had prison art tattooed on both his arms. His nose was so varicose it looked like a road map and his size nineteen neck was covered with so many tattoos V. J. had to look real close to see if he had his head on backwards.

"Well, how about one for me and my friend?"

"Yeah, I guess, but you need to get the monkey out of here."

V. J. saw a sign on the wall that said, "Look Buddy, If You're Enjoying Our TV Show You've Had Too Much To Drink Because We Ain't Got No TV."

A biker, wearing an old German helmet covered with swastikas and built like a fire hydrant, walked over to where V. J. and Macee were standing at the bar. He was wearing a T-shirt with a picture of Panama Jack on the front complete with the eye patch over the cult-classic hero's eye and looked like he had eaten something for supper that was sitting heavy on his stomach.

V. J. thought the biker was suffering from some generational curse and knew he was nearly plastered. *I can't stand to be around somebody sober when I'm drunk and can't stand a drunk when I'm sober.*

The biker, who acted like a dog in a town with no cats, stood there looking as if he had no good on his mind. Then he pointed his finger at V. J. "Who invited you to the party?"

V. J. could see a muscle twitching under the tattoo on his arm.

Some of the other bikers and their women, holding large mugs of beer, gathered around him.

V. J. took a drink of beer. *I'm having a bad dream and I ain't even asleep.*

"We're just thirsty and don't want any trouble," V. J. said as he tried to stare down the biker who looked like a real hooked-up cat.

"This is a private party and I want you out of here, right now, and take those two monkeys with you," the big biker said as Macee stood up straight and glared at him.

V. J. got right in the biker's face. "You could learn a lot from this monkey, he's twice as good, two times as bad and double ugly, just like you. I think we'll stay."

"Well let's see what you got, big talker," the biker said as he threw a punch at him. V. J. ducked just as Macee swung around and kicked the biker in the chest, then spun again and kicked him in the face, knocking him down in front of the bar.

Another biker hit V. J. in the jaw and knocked him down before Macee punched him three times in the face lightning fast, knocking him to the floor.

The next step was as predictable as sin following temptation. The other bikers jumped into the fight and a free-for-all broke out as they ganged up on the two strangers.

About that time a deputy sheriff, who had been drinking with the bikers but had gone to the bathroom to get some relief from the beer, stepped back into the saloon and, when he saw the melee, fired his revolver two times into the ceiling.

Six or seven men were on top of V. J. beating him and several more had Macee cornered near the bar.

"Okay, that's enough! It's over!"

The deputy went over to V. J. and picked him up off the floor.

"You all right, Mister?"

"Yeah, may have lost a couple of teeth. Thanks for your help."

"Ain't nothing to it."

"How about you, young lady?"

"He should never have called me a monkey. Made me mad and besides, I've got a rip in my britches."

"What you guys doin' here?"

"Just passin' through," V. J. replied.

The deputy reached into his pocket. "How about we go feed the jukebox, play a little classic country?"

"I'd just as soon listen to Mozart," Macee said.

"Well, he ain't here tonight," the deputy said.

The deputy slapped V. J. on the back and both men laughed.

After things settled down some, V. J. walked over to the telephone and dialed the Surgeon General's office. The secretary answered. "This is V. J. Casstevens, please let me speak with Dr. Chamberlain."

"One minute please."

"Dr. Casstevens, where are you, we've been worried sick. What happened to your plane and the three agents?"

"The plane crashed and the agents are dead."

"Dead? The agents dead?"

"Someone turned one of the agents. It was Morgan, the pilot. He shot the other two and then got careless and I was able to get away."

"Do you have any idea who could have turned him?"

"No, but he said a man he had never seen before paid him two million in cash to deliver me to an airfield near Chicago. Who do you know in Chicago that might be interested in finding me?"

"Hmm, I can't think of anyone, offhand. How did you get out alive and where are you?"

"That's a long story and I don't even know if I can trust you or anyone else enough to let you know where I am."

"You can trust me, Doctor. We still need to bring you in."

"You know, Mr. Chamberlain, all your plans for bringing me in are about to go sour on my stomach. Every time you send someone to help me something goes wrong. I'm beginning to wonder about who the players are in this thing, and I even wonder about you."

"Now listen, Doctor, don't you ever talk to me like that."

"No, you listen. Two times now you've sent agents to bring me in and all of them are dead."

"You do want us to bring you in."

"I'm not sure. I'll let you know."

"Okay, we'll be waiting for your call."

V. J. hung up the phone and walked back to the table where Macee and Rufus were eating hamburgers.

She saw the worried look on his face. "Big trouble? I wish we could just find a place to hide?"

"There's no place to hide."

V. J. had always heard that a fool learns by experience and a wise man learns by a fool's experience. He vowed that night that he would never be a fool again.

The biker with the Panama Jack T-shirt, accompanied by his girlfriend, a stoner who had moves like an exotic dancer and was holding a copy of Biker Mamas Magazine, came over to their table and sat down. She was so stoned she didn't even know what state she was in.

"Hello," she said with a wet and silky whisper.

V. J. saw she was bad-girl cute and had a blue and gold tattoo on her shoulder that said "Muddah" and her eye shadow had a golden glow. V. J. wondered how dirty, stinking biker types always had such beautiful women, rather than black widow stepmothers or card-cheating New Orleans saloon girls, following them around.

"I'm Panama Jack Rasco, shake the hand of a brand new fool," he said in a somewhat feeble attempt at an apology.

"No sweat," V. J. said as they shook hands.

"Me and my boys are the Black Diamonds out of Atlanta. No bad feelings?"

"Naw, you boys were just having some fun."

"Yeah, but your old lady knocked the fire out of me," the biker said, rubbing his jaw. Come on and I'll introduce you around."

Panama Jack went from table to table introducing V. J. and Macee to the Black Diamonds.

They returned to the table and V. J. asked, "Where you boys headed?"

"We're on our way to Sturgis for the blowout. You just as well saddle up and ride with us."

V. J. had heard about Sturgis, the big biker rally in South Dakota that drew as many as a hundred thousand bikers. *That might be a good place to hide out while I decide what to do.*

"Well, we're sort of on the lam."

"No sweat, man, the law's been after us for years."

V. J. scratched his chin and rubbed his beard. "How much would you charge to loan us a bike to go with you to Sturgis?"

"Nothing man, some of my boys can double up and let you have a bike."

"It's a deal."

"Okay, we leave about eight o'clock in the morning."

After the biker left, Macee asked, "V. J., have you ever ridden a bike?"

"No."

"Oh my."

CHAPTER TWENTY

The next morning the bikers started their Harleys, the motorcycles that supposedly made freedom roar. There were Low Riders, Fat Bobs, Wide Glides, Bad Boys with springer front ends and Hard Tails, with no shock absorbers. There was also a '92 All-Star and a '94 Ultra Tour Guide Classic.

Panama Jack picked a Soft Tail, with suspension under the seat for an easy ride, for V. J. and Macee. He told V. J. to get on the bike and showed him how to kick-start it. When V. J. kicked, the bike took off through the saloon's parking lot, hit a car and ran a quarter of a mile across an open field, with Panama Jack running right along behind, before he could get it stopped.

Panama Jack shook his head. "Okay, you're going to need a little practice." He climbed on the bike behind V. J. and they made several trips around the parking lot.

"I think you got it," Panama Jack said.

The biker gang rode out of the Dutchman's onto Highway 95 and headed northwest toward Kansas City and on to Omaha, Nebraska, where they spent the night in a city park. Just after daybreak the next morning they left for Sturgis.

They crossed the state line into South Dakota where V. J. noticed hundreds of other bikers riding through the magnificent Black Hills, standing like islands in a sea of prairie and grasslands, on their way to the rally.

No one will ever find us with all these bikers around.

He knew the mountains, with sunburned cliffs and rugged ramparts, were sacred to the Sioux and Cheyenne Indians but to him they appeared to have been ruthlessly ravaged by the scouring winds of time and forsaken by the gods.

V. J. looked at the skeletal cliffs and plateaus of the savagely beautiful badlands, reaching upward toward the heavens like an offering. "These are the things post cards are made of."

The bikers passed the Crazy Horse Monument and Mt. Rushmore and as V. J. gazed at the giant sculptures of four of America's greatest heroes he almost laughed out loud as he wondered what it would be like if a fifth person were added to Rushmore and that fifth person would be Macee.

They hit Interstate 90 at Black Hawk City and rode the Harleys wide open. V. J. felt good as he tasted the warm wind that whipped his face. Although he knew a bike was a lonely place, it was a place where a man could tell the truth about himself, forget the melancholy tears and tortured dreams of the past and challenge all the laws of heaven and earth.

"And when I ride down the road, people will have to say, for better or worse, 'A man passed here,'" he told himself as nature screamed his name.

He wasn't sure if it was a blessing or a curse, but he loved the walk on the wild side as a cynical adventurer where there's no fury, no tricks, just magic.

Macee enjoyed every mile as she was able to hug V. J. and she hugged him real tight. Rufus held on behind her.

Wandering the badlands on a bike was like entering another dimension, home of all the legendary soldiers and affable heroes and antiheroes of history, where casket-bearing caissons quietly whisper eulogies to the men who died on a hundred western battlefields, Indians and cavalry and other legends.

Before they arrived in Sturgis, Panama Jack turned back east toward Bear Butte State Park to see the Mato Paha, the Sioux name for Sleeping Bear Mountain. It is a holy place to the plains Indians who still make annual pilgrimages to the sacred mountain to fast, pray and seek vision quests.

"Now let's go to Sturgis!" Panama Jack yelled to his gang.

V. J. had read that the Black Hills Rally is the biggest biker event in the world and the annual Mecca for two weeks for the bikers and their "old ladies." Bikers, who were a counterculture twenty years before the hippies roamed Haight-Asbury in San Francisco in the sixties, frolic in poker runs, drag races, hill climbs, road tours and motorcycle rodeos.

V. J. and Macee were wide-eyed as they pulled up in front of the Road Kill Café, one of the favorite watering holes in Sturgis. V. J. saw a row of "hogs" a half mile long, show bikes, motor cross rigs, glitzy touring cycles, choppers and "rat bikes."

A dozen or more bearded men with potbellies and heavy tattoos stood around in front of the café with their "old ladies," cute girls with limited clothing such as leather halter-tops.

V. J. grinned at Macee. "These gals are not necessarily candidates for Miss America."

They entered the Café where hundreds of bikers milled around drinking beer from large mugs and wearing black leather jackets with decals identifying them from such groups as the Compton Moonshiners,

Market Street Commandos, Bandidos, Yellow Jackets and Hell's Angels.

"I feel safer here than in New Orleans," Macee said.

When the band stepped up on stage and began playing "Proud Mary," Macee wiggled like she was getting ready to shift magnetic poles.

A drunk, with way too many teeth that needed dental work in his smile, staggered over to Macee and tried to dance with her but she politely said no. "Did you have any of those oer d'oeuvres?" he asked. "Those anchovies had a kick to 'em."

"You've had too much to drink."

"First one tonight, with my left hand," he said just before he fell to the floor and passed out.

V. J. saw one biker, who looked like a cadaver half-embalmed with alcohol, pull the life out of a joint with one toke, right there at the bar. He began singing, way off tune, "Sittin' down town in a railroad station, one toke over the line." Then he staggered outside with the full-body dry heaves.

A couple of bikers leaned on the bar and laughed about how they burned a row of outdoor toilets the night before and threw a stick of dynamite at a guy who had the nerve to ride a Honda Gold Wing into the campgrounds. One of them looked like his mind was in another time zone.

A brassy young barmaid, with hungry eyes and small-town sweet, smiled at V. J. "I get off at eleven, if you're interested."

She was a good-natured, amply contoured young lady, all wrapped up like a Christmas package, but V. J. thought the outfit she was wearing was talking way too loud.

"Yeah, maybe I could buy you an ice cream cone."

He was sure she was no more than seventeen and guessed her IQ was smaller than her bust line. "You see I'm kinda hooked up with that big tall girl out there on the dance floor dancing with that ugly biker and I don't think she would understand."

"Okay, catch you later."

Several biker babes, with lots of hair under their armpits, stood at the bar chasing tequila with beer. V.J. thought they must be size eighteen gals looking for love in a size six town. One of them was a big blond that must have weighed two hundred pounds. *I thought trucks like her were built in Detroit. She looks like the kind of woman every mother fears her baby boy will bring home.*

V. J. wondered if the men who had killed the agents would find out they had come to Sturgis. He knew it was a good place to hide and, with his biker's rags and ample beard, he felt secure. But he also knew that having Rufus with them was his biggest problem for not that many people travel with chimps and that alone would make it much easier for someone to find them. But Rufus was family. Then he grinned. "What a family."

Macee stopped dancing and returned to the bar to get a beer.

"We've got to find a room and keep Rufus out of sight," V. J. said.

"Why, he isn't bothering anyone."

"I know Macee, but we need to, oh never mind."

V.J. guessed the bartender was a survivor of many scar-toughened years. "Hey Mac, me and my old lady need a place to stay the night."

"Yeah, what you got in mind?"

"Nothing fancy, just a couple of bunks."

"Well, there's a trailer park called the Jackpyne Village about a mile down the road and I think they still have rooms. But I don't know about the monkey."

"Thanks, man, we'll ease on over that way."

They rode the bike down the road to the trailer park and rented one of the trailers, paying the rent in advance.

Macee turned back the covers and crawled into bed and soon was sound asleep. Rufus curled up at her feet.

V. J. sat down on the couch and closed his eyes. However, he couldn't sleep.

Maybe if we hang out here until this thing is over, we can go back to Atlanta with the Black Diamonds. At least it would be good cover. What about the Surgeon General? There's something strange about that man and I don't like it. I've got to quit calling him. He's going to get me killed.

CHAPTER TWENTY-ONE

D'Angelo keyed his cell phone and dialed Culver-well from the helicopter overlooking the crash site.

"Talk to me, Frankie, any news?"

"Yes, Mr. C., we're in a wooded area about fifty miles north of the Mark Twain National Forest in Missouri. We'll be on the ground in a few minutes and will report back immediately."

"Keep me informed. Dr. Casstevens called the Surgeon General last night from some unknown location but no one has heard from him since."

"We have several search teams on their way in here and the Missouri State Police has offered to help us find the doctor."

"Yes, and time is of the essence. Frankie, I'm sending Bruiser Brown down there to help you look for Casstevens."

"That's good, Mr. C."

Bruiser Brown and the other search teams arrived that afternoon. D'Angelo opened a map and showed them a one-hundred-mile area they would be searching. He also gave them detailed maps of the specific area each team was to cover.

"Now we're going to fan out and find Dr. Casstevens. He and the broad and that monkey did not just disappear off the face of the earth."

He also gave each team a picture of Casstevens. "Check motels and restaurants, convenience stores, gas stations, everywhere, find this man!"

He assigned Bruiser Brown and his partner Tommy Bone to the area just west of the Mark Twain National Park. They checked every business establishment in the area for two days but found nothing. Then, quite by chance, they drove past the Dutchman's.

Bruiser Brown parked the car and they went inside where he showed the bartender the doctor's picture.

"Yeah, that's the man who nearly wrecked this place, him and that long-legged girlfriend of his. And can you believe it, he had a monkey with him."

"When was he here?"

"Well, let me think, okay this is Thursday, he was here Tuesday night and I'll never forget that night. We had a free-for-all and boy it was a good one."

"How long was he here?"

"Just that one night."

"You got any idea where he went?"

"Yeah, to the big biker rally in Sturgis."

"Sturgis?"

"The biker blowout in South Dakota."

"You're sure?"

"Saw him with my own eyes. He was riding a Harley with his girlfriend on behind and that monkey behind her."

"You're positive there was a monkey."

"Yeah, that monkey stunk like a skunk and drank two six packs of beer in one setting, never seen nothing like it."

Bruiser Brown thanked the bartender, gave him a twenty and returned to the car where he dialed D'Angelo on his cell phone.

"Yeah, Frankie."

"We got a lead on Dr. Casstevens."

"All right! Where is he?"

"You ever heard of Sturgis?"

"Yeah, my kid brother went out there a couple of times."

"Well, a bartender at a place called the Dutchman's said he saw the doctor and his girlfriend leave for Sturgis two days ago. And guess what, he had the chimp with him."

"Hmm, okay Bruiser, just stand by and I'll call you back in a few minutes."

D'Angelo dialed Culverwell's private phone.

"This is Culverwell."

"Boss we have a lead on the doctor."

"That's good, Frankie, where is he?"

"He hooked up with a motorcycle gang on their way the Black Hills Rally in Sturgis, South Dakota."

"That Dr. Casstevens is one cagey fellow. Where did he meet up with the biker gang?"

"At a country saloon in Missouri."

"How long has he been gone?"

"About two days."

"Okay, Frankie, you know what to do. Bring him to me."

D'Angelo called Bruiser Brown. "I want you to meet me at an old deserted army base about fifteen miles south of St. Louis tomorrow morning. There is a landing strip down there that was used in World War II. I'm sure some of the locals can tell you how to get there."

"You want Bone?"

"No, send him back to Chicago."

Bruiser Brown arrived at the airstrip before daylight. About an hour later D'Angelo's plane landed, picked him up and headed for Sioux Falls, South Dakota.

D'Angelo explained the plan to Bruiser Brown and

Tom Greene, the pilot.

"When we arrive in Sioux Falls, Bruiser and I will rent a car and go on to Sturgis. We'll hang out, drink a couple of beers and get a feel for the place. Then we'll make our move and see if we can locate the doctor and the broad -- and the chimp."

Greene asked for and received clearance from the Sioux Falls tower to land on an auxiliary runway. He also asked the controller where he could park the plane and the controller directed him to Hangar Number Six.

Green taxied up to the hangar and killed his engines. Two men opened the large sliding doors and pulled the jet inside.

D'Angelo and Bruiser Brown arrived in Sturgis and went into the Dry Gulch Saloon and cased the joint. They also dropped into the Armadillo Restaurant and ate dinner, then went on to the Crazy Horse Saloon and finally to the Thunder One Café, but found no one who had seen Casstevens.

That night they rented a room but neither of them could sleep.

The next morning they returned to the strip and continued checking out the crowds of bikers and their babes.

About noon D'Angelo decided to start asking questions. They visited a dozen bars and restaurants asking the bartenders and waiters if they had seen Casstevens and his girlfriend and noted that they would have had a pet chimpanzee with them.

They worked most of the day and after dark went in the Road Kill Café and walked up to the bar.

"What will you have, gents?" the bartender asked.

"How about a beer?" D'Angelo asked.

They drank several beers and asked the bartender,

whose name was Fred, all about Sturgis and the rally
and even inquired about how long the Road Kill Café
had been in business.

"We came right in here with the Gypsies."

"The who?"

"Jackpyne Gypsies. They started the rally back in the
thirties. Been going ever since."

"Really?"

"They weren't real gypsies, just took the name."

"Well Fred, me and my buddy heard the wildest
story the other night. Something about a monkey coming in here and drinking a six-pack of beer."

"Yeah, served the monkey myself."

"Well, I sure would like to meet a monkey that
could drink a six-pack of beer. You reckon that monkey's still around?"

"Could be. Was with some bearded guy and a broad
and they went to a trailer park about a mile down the
street. Place called the Jackpyne Village."

"You have just made my day." D'Angelo handed
the bartender a twenty. "I sure want to meet that monkey."

They left the café, drove about a mile to the Jackpyne Village and parked in front of the manager's office.

D'Angelo went inside, rang a bell and the manager
entered through a back door.

"Good evening, need a room?"

"No, I'm trying to locate my brother-in-law Victor
Casstevens."

"We have no Cassstevens here."

"Well, sometimes he uses other names, especially
when he's running around on my sister, if you know
what I mean. And he may have a monkey with him."

"Why you trying to find him?"

"His mother is dying, only has a few more days to live. She said she wants to see Victor before she dies."

"Well the man with the monkey said his name is John Smith and he didn't give me the woman's name. And yeah, he has got a monkey with him."

"Would it be possible for me to talk with him about his mother?"

"Sure, he's in number eight down the street."

"Thank you, Sir, his mother will say a prayer for you."

They drove past number eight and parked.

D'Angelo checked his Glock Nine Millimeter pistol. "Bruiser, I'm going in by myself. I want you to cover the back door in case they run."

"You got it, Boss."

D'Angelo walked up to the front of number eight and knocked on the door.

"V. J., somebody's at the door," Macee said as she stepped into the bathroom and closed the door.

"Who is it?"

"The manager, I need to talk to you."

When V. J. opened the door, D'Angelo stuck his Nine Millimeter in his stomach. "We meet at last, Dr. Casstevens," he said with a crazy look of shadows in his eyes.

V. J.'s blood froze. "Who are you and what do you want?" V. J. asked the clinched-jawed man with a chilling grin and cold, probing eyes.

"All in due time."

Macee flushed the toilet, opened the bathroom door and screamed when she saw D'Angelo holding a gun on V. J.

"V. J., who is this man?"

"I don't know."

D'Angelo opened the back door and motioned for Bruiser Brown to come into the trailer.

Rufus got so excited he jumped up and swung from the light fixture, farted twice then peed all over Bruiser Brown's shoes.

"I'll kill that monkey!"

"Settle down, Bruiser," D'Angelo said.

V. J. put his arm around Rufus and tried to calm him down. He glanced over at Bruiser Brown and thought this guy is a one-man gang who looks about half tough, maybe more.

"Now, Doctor, we can do this the easy way or the hard way," D'Angelo said. "Just remember that a bullet moving at fifteen-hundred feet per second can ruin your day but, on the other hand, it'll cure all your diseases."

"I don't like that kind of talk, do something!" Macee said.

V. J. put his arm around her. "Settle down."

D'Angelo glared at V. J. "You can either cooperate and enjoy a very comfortable flight or we can gag you and keep you tied up. What will it be?"

"Flight to where?"

"You'll find out soon enough."

This guy is beginning to sound like a Greek messenger.

He glanced over at Macee who was wide-eyed with fear. "Don't worry, we're going to be okay."

"V. J., I can't even go to the toilet without somebody bustin' in here with a gun. This is major annoying."

"You're lucky, Dr. Casstevens, maybe even charmed, considering all you have been through," D'Angelo said. "I'd like to follow you around the race track a couple of times."

Then he stepped out on the front porch and dialed Culverwell.

"This is Frankie."

"Is the news good?"

"Yes, Mr. C., the news is good. We have Dr. Casstevens in custody."

"Good Frankie, and when will you have him back in Chicago?"

"Sometime early in the morning."

"Yes, and every minute counts."

After they were airborne, D'Angelo untied their hands and let them roam freely about the cabin. Bruiser Brown prepared some sandwiches and coffee.

V. J. wondered how they found him. *It had to be Rufus, yeah. They must have learned we left with the bikers and all they had to do was follow us to Sturgis. Then it was easy. I'm the only guy out here with a monkey.*

After they ate the sandwiches, V. J. asked D'Angelo, "Now can you tell us where we are going?"

"Yeah, why not, our destination is Chicago."

"Chicago?"

"Well that will be kinda nice, because I've never been to Chicago," Macee said as a tear dripped off her cheek. She wished V. J. would hold her and tell her that everything's going to be all right.

V. J. squeezed her hand. "Yeah, I'm sure it's going to be real nice."

"You know something, V. J., we're the best team since Bonnie and Clyde."

He smiled but did not reply.

"V. J., you're going to make a widow out of me before you ever get a chance to marry me."

"Who said I was going to marry you?"

"Oh, I don't know, I was just thinking."

She took a pencil out of her purse and scribbled something on a note pad. When she finished, she handed it to V. J.

"I'm lost and gone to look for myself. If anyone sees me coming back before I get there, please tell me where I am and where I've been."

Then she put her head on V. J.'s shoulder and wept.

V. J. knew that in her own simple way Macee had entered a fantasy world where lovers cry and poets dream and that she soon would be sound asleep. And he would be there with her all through the night and with her when she wakes up the next morning.

CHAPTER TWENTY-TWO

Agent Greene landed the Culverwell jet at Chicago's Meigs Field on Northerly Island across the harbor from Lake Shore Drive, taxied the plane to a small hangar and cut the engines.

V. J. looked out the window and saw a long, black limousine drive up beside the plane.

The pilot opened the door and lowered the stairs. "Okay, Frankie, you're good to go."

"Thanks, Tom, good job."

Bruiser Brown politely helped V. J. and Macee into the limo and the driver headed toward Solidarity Drive and into the Chicago business district.

They drove through the crowded streets moving in and out of traffic and dodging pedestrians.

V. J knew a lot of bad things had ganged up on him and Macee. But he feared the worst may be yet to come.

They arrived at the Culverwell Building on Michigan Avenue. The driver stopped and opened the back door.

"Okay, Doctor, let's go," D'Angelo said as he helped him and Macee out of the limo and to the front door as Rufus trailed along behind.

The uniformed guards at the entrance nodded to D'Angelo and Bruiser Brown as they passed the checkpoint on the way to the elevator. They stepped inside and D'Angelo pressed the button that said "Penthouse."

The elevator door opened. "Follow me," D'Angelo

said.

V. J. had never seen such luxury, with the deep carpets and paintings by Monet, Degas and Pablo Picasso on the walls.

"Get a load of these digs," V. J. told Macee as he looked all around the room at the antique furniture, silver settings and ornate sculptures and bronze busts of Julius Caesar, Alexander the Great and Napoleon. There was also a beautiful display of European art and a wildlife diorama on the wall.

"V. J., this place is nicer than Williams Funeral Parlor down in Bogalusa. That's where we buried Grandma Geneva."

V. J. smiled, squeezed her hand and walked over to the window. He looked out at the jagged Chicago skyline and saw heavy traffic moving along Lake Shore Drive and waves breaking fifty yards out in Lake Michigan and moving slowly toward the shore. *By what terrible trickery of fate did we ever wind up here?*

"Dr. Casstevens, can I get you and your lady something, a drink, anything?" Bruiser Brown asked.

"Yeah, maybe some coffee, cream and sugar, and one for the chimp."

Bruiser Brown returned with the coffee and Macee handed a cup to Rufus who grunted.

A few minutes later Frankie D'Angelo entered the room. "Mr. Culverwell will see you momentarily."

V. J. nodded. "Thank you."

Culverwell entered the room in his wheelchair. "Mr. C, this is Dr. Victor Casstevens and his friend Macee Marineaux, and I believe he calls the chimp Rufus," D'Angelo said.

"It's good to finally meet you, Doctor," Culverwell said, sucking hard for air to breathe. "You are my guests here and I want to assure you that you are in no danger whatsoever."

"Well, these are very strained circumstances and I don't appreciate being kidnapped at gunpoint."

"Oh, you will understand sooner than later that the urgency of our actions was based on absolute necessity." Culverwell struggled with each word.

V. J. guessed the old man was in his seventies. He had heavy brows, a cleft chin and hair shot with gray. His whiskers were beyond the shadow stage but too short for a beard and there was a network of fine lines gathered at the contours of his eyes, eyes like holes in the furnace of hell. And he looked weak and pale.

I've seen mummies that look happier than this guy and he's not exactly an elder in the Presbyterian Church.

V. J. studied the look on the seemingly harmless old man's face and the inflection of his words and wondered if he was a mad man, the custodian of some dark and inscrutable secret.

"Doctor, we've followed your work for a number of years as you have searched for the elusive magic bullet that would unlock the mystery of aging," Culverwell said, sounding like his voice was dipped in poison with a conscience crying out for absolution. "And now we are very interested in the most recent results of that research."

"Thank you for your interest but my research may require many years of further testing to determine exactly what I have found, or perhaps I should say what was given to me by powers not my own."

"Well, it seems quite encouraging to me."

Culverwell explained that some twenty years earlier his doctors diagnosed him with a rare autoimmune disease and said he would live only a year. "But I decided to challenge the disease and fight back. At least I'm still alive these many years later but I've been destined to travel a lonely road."

"That takes a great deal of courage."

"I have greatly admired you who are working to conquer the ultimate disease that has haunted humanity since the beginning of time. In our search for the answer for the mystery of aging we have monitored every research center in the land and several overseas. I have already spent more than three hundred million dollars in this pursuit and, until you entered the equation, found little of substance."

"Actually, Sir, my research could prove to be more conjecture than substance."

"You know, my men placed the hidden cameras in your office the week before you arrived in New Orleans and we have followed your work these ten years. We have thousands of hours of video tapes of your research and experiments in our files. But frankly, Doctor, there really wasn't that much work or research."

"I never detected the presence of the camera in my office. Your people must be real pros. But I guess for three hundred mil you can hire the best."

"Most of the surveillance of your work was quite disappointing for you are, as they say, something of a maverick scientist. But the final experiment with your chimpanzee made all of our efforts worthwhile and now we want to help you bring your scientific genius to fruition. It gives me hope that one day I will be able to lift myself up out of this wheelchair. You know, Doctor, I've tried to suppress the terrors of aging for they are so frightening, particularly in the long night hours when the penthouse fills up with silence and I am able to stay only a heartbeat ahead of my worst fears."

Culverwell turned his wheelchair around and faced D'Angelo. "Now Frankie, I want you to entertain Ms. Marineaux for a few hours while I speak privately with Dr. Casstevens and you can take the chimpanzee Rufus with you. Perhaps she would like to go shopping for some new clothes. Let her have anything she wants for we desire to make her stay here enjoyable."

"V. J., wha — "

"It's okay, Macee, you will be safe with Mr. D'Angelo. Go ahead and buy some new clothes, it'll make you feel better."

"I'd rather stay here with you," she said as D'Angelo took her by the arm and led her toward the elevator.

Culverwell removed the oxygen tubes from his nose, took a bottle of medicine from a nearby table, sprayed both of his nostrils, and replaced the tubes.

"How does it feel, Doctor, to wake up one morning and find yourself in the center of history?"

"I really hadn't thought about it, and the idea may be undeserved."

"Oh no, it is well deserved and I applaud your genius. You may have tipped the scales between man and nature for supremacy of the world."

"I've certainly never been called a genius before."

"Doctor, it must be very obvious to you that I am dying and I need your help," Culverwell said with a stoic face of tragedy. " I know one day I must cross the dark river of death and the river is mean and I want to avoid it as long as possible."

"I'm not sure I can help you."

"Oh, I think you can."

V. J. decided to hedge his bet. "Mr. Culverwell, I may have discovered a way to somewhat renew the life of a chimpanzee, but I have no idea if it will work on a human being. It's even possible that there could be a severe reaction to the treatment."

"That's a risk I am perfectly willing to take. I don't have any other options and this new millennium is very rapidly spinning us into the future."

V. J. looked out the window at the waters of Lake Michigan. *Oh how I wish I was back in New Orleans with Macee, just hanging out in the Quarter, going to Mardi Gras, eating etouffe and drinking beer in the hiding place with Rufus. What a good life I once had.*

Without warning the old man began to cough and gag and gasp for breath and then went into a convulsion. V. J. could see his face turning blue. Bruiser Brown rushed into the room, picked him up out of the wheelchair and hit him several times on the back until he breathed again.

Bruiser Brown turned to V. J. "Dr. Casstevens, Mr. Culverwell will need some rest. We will call you when he is ready to resume the discussion."

He wheeled the old man out of the room and V. J. went to find Macee.

CHAPTER TWENTY-THREE

Detectives Dula and Francis arrived at O'Hare Airport and hailed a taxi to take them downtown to meet with Detective Captain Pat O'Reilly of the Chicago Police Department's Criminal Intelligence Division. Dula called O'Reilly before departing from New Orleans and the Captain informed him he had a rap sheet on Healy John Hurt, whose partial fingerprint was found at the Research Center after the killings.

The taxi pulled up in front of Central Police Station and they hurried inside. "I'm Lieutenant Dula and this is Detective Francis from the New Orleans PD and we're here to see Captain O'Reilly," Dula told the desk sergeant.

"Yeah, the Captain has been expecting you," the sergeant replied, then buzzed his office.

A few minutes later Captain O'Reilly, a big, lantern-jawed man with a perpetual frown on his face, came to the sergeant's desk. "Gentlemen, welcome to Chicago."

Dula shook hands with the Captain. "Thank you for taking time to help us. We're here in connection with the killings in New Orleans a few days ago."

"Yeah, I read about it, and you think there may be a Chicago connection?"

"Could be, we picked up a print from a Healy John Hurt, the guy I mentioned to you on the phone. We thought you might be able to tell us a little more about him."

The Captain went to his filing cabinet and lifted Hurt's rap sheet. "Maybe this will help you."

The detectives studied the rap sheet and noticed Hurt had been in trouble with the law since he was a teenager growing up on the south side of Chicago.

"I guess this is his last-known address?" Francis asked.

"Yeah, I had one of my men check him out and he's living in a high rise on North State. You think he's tied in to the killings?"

"We don't know, Captain, but he's the only lead we have," Dula said.

"The guy has been clean for the last several years. He works for Tower Enterprises a subsidiary of the Culverwell Company," the Captain said. "Tower manages a couple dozen big properties downtown."

"Ever had any trouble with them?" Francis asked.

"No, occasionally we hear rumors of muscle being used when the contracts are re-negotiated with some of the tenants, but no one has ever called us in on it."

"What about Culverwell?" Dula asked.

"Alexander Culverwell may be the richest man in Chicago, into steel, railroads, soft-drink franchises, and he owns hundreds of properties all over Chicago. Years ago he moved in all the high society circles, then suddenly dropped from sight and became something of a recluse."

"Captain, any possibility we could get a tap on Hurt's phone?" Dula asked.

"Considering the gravity of the situation, I believe the judge will grant a tap. We'll try for the court order. And I'll send one of our surveillance teams out there to help you. They'll be in a commercial van that says Big

Shi Plumbing on the side. You can join them tonight."

"Thank you, Captain, we'll keep in touch."

The detectives checked into a downtown hotel and Dula called Chief Landry in New Orleans.

"Yeah, this is Landry."

"Chief, we're in the Sherman Hotel, Room 1201 and we've already made contact with Chicago PD. They are getting a court order for a wiretap on Healy John Hurt's phone and should have a surveillance team in place before long. We'll join them this evening."

"Okay, Lieutenant, you know we really need to turn something, the people down here are going crazy since a local radio jock spread the rumor that there are some mass murderers loose on the streets of New Orleans. Hang in there and maybe we'll get a break."

"Ten-four, Chief."

About mid-afternoon Bruiser Brown wheeled the old man back into the penthouse meeting room to resume his discussion with V. J. who noticed that some of the color had returned to the old man's sallow face.

"So we meet again, Dr. Casstevens. I trust our time together will be very productive."

V. J. decided to change the conversation and ask some probing questions to see if Culverwell felt any culpability for the murders his men committed.

"Why was it necessary to kill all the people at the Center and the agents?"

"Your colleagues went crazy and my men had no other choice but to eliminate them, otherwise all of my work would have been in jeopardy," Culverwell replied angrily, revealing he was capable of mercurial mood shifts. "And the agents, they were expendable, just government lackeys who were paid killers themselves. And besides, they knew their jobs were dangerous."

"But any death, your death, theirs, is so final."

Culverwell did not respond but his voice mellowed as he continued. "Actually, Doctor, we in America are infected with superstition and surrounded by lovers, liars and thieves. And I have a vision of a much better world and the elimination of mongrel humanity is a giant first step toward a utopia here on earth."

V. J. raised his eyes toward the high penthouse ceiling and silently prayed, "God, somebody up there needs to check this out because I'm really in a mess down here."

"None is sacrosanct, no, not one."

"But Mr. Culverwell, the agents had wives and children who were left behind. What about them?"

"I consider it a sacrifice of these men of lower estate for the common good of the upper estate and hence for all mankind. The FBI men are themselves experts in the elimination of innocents who get in their way and they call it collateral damage. No, you'll not find me bleating *mea culpas* or manipulative tears for their lives."

"But why was it necessary to kill them? They were good men doing a thankless job and there probably will never even be a brief footnote in a history book to mark their passing."

"Desperate people do desperate things and no man who holds great power in his hands can allow lesser men to crush his dreams," Culverwell said, clearly revealing the arrogance that money brings. "A hunter never apologizes to the prey. And Doctor, you and I both know that man is a hunter."

V. J. thought about what Culverwell said. *This guy is trying to act like a god or a demigod and his dreams are too much like nightmares to suit me.*

"People do crazy things without being crazy," V. J. said with compassion. "Sure, you've had some bad things laid on your table and certain agonies that don't seem to want to go away. But that does not justify taking the lives of others."

"Dr. Cassstevens, we all suffer from the same disease of growing old, and do you have any idea what it is like to be held hostage by frailties of the flesh?" Culverwell asked, with a hint of sadness in his voice. "It is something akin to other realities like hunger, thirst, pain and suffering. Your eyes don't focus like they once did and your pain keeps you awake at night."

V. J. suddenly realized Culverwell had a pathological disrespect for life, at least all life except his own. *He has lost touch with the blind history of the universe, a history that says men live and die and are followed by other men who live and die and that's just the way it is. But if, and I must emphasize if, I have found a way to break that chain of history then what am I to do with a sociopath like Culverwell?*

"Mr. Culverwell, exactly why have you brought me here and what do you want?"

"Of course you realize, Doctor, that death is never in anybody's plans, it just happens, unless you can defeat it, otherwise it recycles every man back to the earth. So I want you to help me turn back death. You know what Woody Allen says, 'Eternity is very long, especially toward the end,' and I was never bred to keep my expectations low. You know, I once had a near-death experience."

"Oh, tell me about it," V. J. said, thinking the old man was just a step away from rigor.

"There was no tunnel, no light, no creatures in white, just nags and hags and furry creatures that kept biting at me and calling me names. It was like being chased down a road to nowhere with no one to rescue me. Actually, Doctor, I believe I looked into the jaws of death and saw my own face and the gates of hell opened up and the demons of death attacked me. I hope to outlive that memory."

V. J. realized the old man was having great difficulty in separating truth from reality. "Memories have a very hard edge."

"What a relief when you return from the unknown world to the real world where dreams keep you warm as life grows colder. And you are grateful that some unknown force came to slay the dragons and keep the monsters away."

"I've never been to the unknown world." *This guy is right for all the wrong reasons and he is desperate to buy back some time from Mother Nature and say hello to tomorrow. But he feels no responsibility for any of his actions and the ability to feel guilt is all that separates any of us from psychopaths.*

Culverwell shifted in his wheelchair. "Actually fear is what we are all about and not guilt but I plan to do a lot more living before the last door slams on my life, even as the past tugs at me like Marley's ghost. There will be no sense of guilt for guilt is a ghost that haunts its own house."

Culverwell removed the oxygen tubes from his nose, wheezed and sprayed each nostril again, then replaced the tubes. He forced his ruined lungs to draw in air and exhale it as his brown-spotted hands shook under the curse of morphine that made the tubes bearable. His time seemed measured in dying breaths and V. J. suspected his next trip to the hospital could be his last.

"You know, Doctor, regret is an inevitable consequence of life and when you reach old age you are disappointed that life is so short."

"But, Sir, it's endemic to human nature. We are born, we live and we die."

"Yes, but life creates a certain ambience and always saves the best for last for it is when we are old and wise that we learn the answers to the deepest mysteries of the universe. When the focus that gives the mind its power turns against you, faith grows weak and doubt and fear take its place. That's where I am right now and that is why I need you. The end, with a new beginning, is where we must start."

"But you don't understand, I'm not sure I can give you, or anyone, a new beginning," V. J. said, realizing the old man was about to lose his dream, the last thing holding him together. "I need to do more research to fully understand the premature results I have experienced."

Culverwell sighed and looked at his watch. "Doctor Casstevens, I'm tired and must retire for the evening. I'll probably not sleep that much because I sit in the dark and dream dreams for hours each night. We'll meet again tomorrow morning. Good night."

He rang a bell and Bruiser Brown entered the room, turned the wheelchair around and escorted him to his sleeping quarters.

V. J. glanced at his watch and saw that it was 8 p.m. He and Alexander Culverwell had been talking for nearly six hours.

Bruiser Brown returned and escorted V. J. to a penthouse bedroom and told him Macee was next door.

He knocked on Macee's door and told her everything that he and Culverwell had discussed.

Macee was anxious to show him all the new clothes she had purchased. "And I bought a pair of striped overalls and railroad engineer's cap for Rufus."

V. J. grinned when he saw Rufus in the overalls, wearing the cap and smoking a cigar. "Good boy, Rufus, you and Macee are my two best friends."

Macee saw his hand trembling and wrapped her arms around him. "V. J., it's going to be okay. We've made it through some tough times and we'll make it through this."

After dark Dula and Francis caught a taxi and headed for North State Street. They asked the driver to stop a block away from Hurt's high-rise then walked to the van, with "Big Shi Plumbing" painted on either side, that was parked about a block away from the subject's building.

Dula rapped on the back door and one of the detectives inside opened it. "You Dula and Francis?"

"Yeah," Dula said.

"Come on in, I'm Franco and this is Martinez," the man said, reaching out to shake hands with the detectives.

"Thanks for giving us a hand. This is my partner Charlie Francis."

Dula observed the van was equipped with state-of-the-art surveillance and listening devices. Detective Martinez had on a set of earphones and was monitoring all the calls going in and out of the subject's home.

"Nothing yet," Martinez said. "The guy called a few of his friends to come over to play poker, and ordered pizza, that's it."

About midnight another call came in and this time Detective Martinez motioned for Dula to take the headphones.

Dula listened intently as the caller said, "Healy John,

this is Frankie."

"What's going on, my man?"

"Need some help, Mr. C wants you to round up a few of the boys and be at the Culverwell Institute tomorrow morning at 8 a.m."

"What's going down, Frankie?"

"I'll explain it to you tomorrow morning."

After D'Angelo hung up the phone, Dula saw the poker players leave Hurt's home.

A few minutes later Hurt began calling several men telling them to meet him at the Institute the next morning. Detective Martinez wrote down all the phone numbers, relayed them downtown to CID and asked for a make on each of the men. A few minutes later the sergeant on duty at CID called Martinez and gave him a profile on the ten men Hurt had called.

"These are some bad boys," the sergeant said. "A couple of them have done time for manslaughter, two more for armed robbery and guess what, three of them have been mercenaries in Africa."

"Can I presume the Mr. C is Culverwell?" Dula asked Franco.

"Yeah, makes sense."

"What Institute they talking about?"

"Some years ago Alexander Culverwell spent two hundred million dollars building a state-of-the-art scientific center across the street from the University of Chicago down on the south side," Franco explained. "I'll get an unmarked car out here and you can tail Hurt when he leaves the house to make sure we don't lose him, and I'll request a chopper."

"Thanks, Franco."

Dula sat down beside Francis. "When we first arrived I wondered if we were on a wild goose chase and connecting this guy Hurt to the killings in New Orleans was a long-shot. But now we may have a break."

Francis nodded. "Yeah, I hope we can nail this guy and all the others who killed our people in New Orleans."

Another Chicago detective arrived before daylight and introduced himself to Dula and Francis. "I'm Toots Koplinski, CID. The Captain wants me to give you boys a hand."

"I'm Scott Dula from New Orleans and this is Charlie Francis." They both shook hands with the officer.

"The desk sergeant said we were to tail some guy named Hurt."

"Yeah, he lives down the block and is supposed to go to the Culverwell Institute early this morning," Franco explained. "I've got a chopper standing by to tail him in case he makes us."

At exactly 6 a. m. the garage door of the high-rise building opened and a man believed to be Hurt drove south on State Street toward downtown Chicago, turned back east on East Jackson Drive to Lakeshore then south toward the Institute. The detectives followed at a safe distance.

They tailed the subject for about a mile when Detective Koplinski keyed his radio and said, "Air Eagle Dispatch, this is car forty-eight, you copy?"

"This is Air Eagle Dispatch, go ahead car forty-eight."

"We're tailing a subject down Lakeshore Drive and request chopper surveillance."

"What's your twenty?"

"We're on Lakeshore about a mile south of Jackson tailing a subject driving a blue Crown Victoria."

"Ten-four, car forty-eight, we're on our way."

About ten minutes later Dula spotted the helicopter high above the subject's car.

"Car forty-eight, this is Georgie Boy with Air Eagle Ten, we have the subject in sight."

"Good show, Air Eagle Ten, we want you to keep your eyes on this bad boy," Koplinski said.

"Ten-four," the pilot, replied.

The subject continued south on Lakeshore for several miles, passed the 49th Street Beach and the Museum of Science and Industry then took a right on 55th Street and headed toward the University of Chicago. When he reached Midway Plaisance Street, which runs right down the middle of the University, he took a left, drove to the end of the street and pulled into the parking lot of the Culverwell Research Institute.

As they approached the campus, Dula remembered the University was known as the birthplace of nuclear energy because of the Manhattan Project during World War II.

Koplinski keyed his radio. "Car forty-eight to Air Eagle Ten, you copy?"

"Go ahead car forty-eight."

"The subject has arrived at his twenty and thank you for hanging in there with us."

"That's a big ten-four, call us if you need us," the pilot said, then banked the chopper and flew away.

Detective Koplinski parked the unmarked car a block away from the Institute where they could get a clear view of any activity in the area.

"There it is, the Culverwell Institute, ten floors of nothing but steel and glass surrounded by the most beautiful landscape in all of Chicago."

"Yeah, it's impressive," Francis said.

Dula opened the car door. "Hey, Koplinski, I'm going up the street to a pay phone and call the Chief, be right back."

"Bring us some coffee and doughnuts," Francis said.

"Yeah buddy."

Dula walked along the street where he saw hundreds of students on their way to class. *These kids are oblivious to what may be going down here today, something that could be as important as the Manhattan Project, maybe more important.*

He found a phone, dialed police headquarters in New Orleans and asked for Chief Landry.

"Who's calling, please?" the secretary asked.

"This is Lieutenant Dula in Chicago."

The Chief picked up the phone. "Scott, talk to me, give me some good news."

"We got a break, Chief, we believe something big is going down and it may involve Dr. Casstevens. We tapped Healy John Hurt's phone and Culverwell's chief of security called him last night and told him to round up a bunch of the boys."

"Okay, so where does that leave us?"

"Looks like they need some muscle at the Institute which is down near the University of Chicago on the city's south side."

"What makes you think Casstevens will show up?"

"I believe Culverwell has Casstevens and is going to set him up in the Institute to do some research. It's the only connection we have to Healy's print showing up in the Center in New Orleans."

"Sounds like a long shot to me."

"Now stay with me, Chief. I've been piecing a few things together. Culverwell is a billionaire recluse who has been sick for twenty years and may be about ready to croak. Could be he wants Casstevens to pull some rabbit out of the hat and save him."

"That's pure speculation."

"Yeah, Chief, but I've got a hunch and if I'm right, Dr. Casstevens is going to show up here."

"Then what are you going to do?"

"The Chicago PD has a SWAT team standing by. They'll help us take him."

"Okay, Scott, you and Charlie be careful and remember that there's no scientist in the world worth getting killed over."

"Yeah, I know."

"And Scott, you boys are doing a fine piece of police work and I'm proud of you. Wish I was there with you."

"Thanks, Chief, I'll keep in touch." Dula hung up the phone and went to a convenience store on the corner to pick up some coffee and doughnuts.

When he returned to the unmarked police car, Francis told him several of Healy's men had shown up at the Institute. A few minutes later, a second carload arrived. "That makes an even dozen."

"Some heavy muscle," Dula said.

"Yeah, those are some bad boys," Koplinski replied.

Dula pulled off his coat and tie. "Boys, I'm going to take a walk around the building and see what's going on."

"We'll hang out here," Francis said.

Dula walked past the entrance to the Institute where he saw men and women entering the building wearing white lab coats and noticed two uniformed security guards at the entrance. An eight-foot bronze statue of Alexander Culverwell stood in front of the building. He saw three men on the roof with binoculars carefully scanning the surrounding area.

He returned to the car a couple of hours later.

You boys hungry?" Koplinski asked.

"Yeah, real hungry," Francis replied.

"Okay, there's a vendor up the street, makes great hot dogs, a lot of the college kids hang out there. I'll pick up something for you guys."

"Thanks, Toots," Dula said.

Koplinski returned with the hotdogs and several large cups of coffee. Dula ate the hotdog and drank the coffee and thought how tedious and time-consuming police work can be. *Here we are eating hot dogs and the bad guys are probably in fancy restaurants having a nice wine, filet mignon and lobster, and cherries jubilee. Maybe this is the price a man pays for doing something that is right and living with a clean conscience.*

Avanzini's man in New Orleans, who was monitoring Chief Landry's telephone calls, contacted him immediately after the Chief spoke with Dula.

"Mr. Avanzini, this is Georgio Boudreaux, I've been helping Captain Blaine monitor the tap you asked for. The Captain told me to call you if I picked up anything of importance."

"Yeah, go ahead Georgio."

"Well, it looks like your man Casstevens is in Chicago and may be on his way to the south side sometime in the near future. Chief Landry got a call about ten minutes ago from one Lieutenant Scott Dula on assignment in Chicago, apparently looking for the doctor."

"Yeah, go on."

"According to Dula, he believes that a man by the name of Alexander Culverwell, a Chicago billionaire, has grabbed Casstevens and plans to take him to his Research Institute on the south side near Chicago University real soon."

"Anything else?"

"Yeah, Dula said a SWAT team is standing by to rescue Doctor Casstevens if he shows up."

"Thank you, Georgio, call me if anything else starts
to go down."

"Yes Sir, Mr. Avanzini."

Just before dark Healy and his men came out of the
Institute, loaded into several cars and drove away.

"Do we need to follow them?" Koplinski asked.

"No, I think there's been a hitch of some kind and
Casstevens didn't show up but I have a hunch we are in
the right place so let's hang here the rest of the night,"
Dula replied. "If I'm right, they'll be back tomorrow
morning."

A few minutes later Koplinski received a call from
Central Dispatch. "Car forty-eight, this is central, what's
your twenty?"

"About a block north of the Culverwell Institute
near the University campus."

"Captain O'Reilly is sending Detective Jack Banion
to relieve you for the night."

"That's a big ten-four."

"What about the boys from New Orleans?"

Dula motioned to the officer that they would keep
up the surveillance during the night.

"They're set for the night, so send Happy Jack on
down."

"Ten-four, Central Dispatch out."

Detective Jack Banion arrived about thirty minutes
later to continue the surveillance with Dula and Francis.

"Jack, this is Detective Francis and Lieutenant Dula
of the New Orleans PD," Koplinski said as he intro-

duced the men. "And fellows, this is Happy Jack Banion, twenty-year veteran of the CID, and one bad dude
when he gets jammed up."

"Good to meet you," Banion said, extending his
hand. "You boys are a long way from home,"

"Yeah, thanks for coming down to help us," Dula
said.

"No sweat."

Dula and Francis took turns sleeping in the back
seat of the police car during the night but there was no
movement of any kind at the Institute.

Avanzini knew a Chicago mob boss named Mario
Balducci who owed him several favors so he decided to
give him a call.

"Yeah Luka, this is Mario. This must be something
big for me to get a call from Luka Avanzini."

"I need your help, Mario, and it's big."

"I owe you, so yeah, if I can help."

Luka explained that he needed detailed maps of
Chicago University and the surrounding area and schematics of the building permits of the Culverwell Research Institute.

"And we're probably going to need a good torch,"
Avanzini said.

"Yeah, I use one of my own boys."

"Charter a plane and get the maps and schematics to
New York as soon as you have them in hand."

"It may take a while. The maps will be easy, but I'll
have to send my men to the city engineer's office to pick
up the schematics of the Institute."

"Okay, but make sure I have them today."

"Yeah, Luka, do you mind telling me what this is all
about?"

"Maybe later."

Mario Balducci's courier arrived in New York City at 7 p. m. that evening by chartered jet and delivered the maps of the University of Chicago area and the schematics of the Culverwell Institute to Avanzini.

He called his men together. "You are my most trusted men and the Avanzini family has always been able to count on you and together we have built a great empire. But without you it would have been impossible. I have called on you many times in the past and you have always been there for the family. Today I call on you again."

Then he explained their mission. "There is a scientist from New Orleans who has made a discovery that might help my aging father Rocko Avanzini. We must go to Chicago and find him and it may be dangerous for he is being held by some powerful men."

He spread maps of the area around the University and the schematics of the Culverwell Institute building out on a large table. "Now these maps show you the layouts of the building we're going to hit. Here's how it's going to play out."

He paused for a minute and looked around the room. *These guys would walk into the jaws of hell for me and my father and it is men like this that make life worth living.*

"Okay, we've got a lot of work to do, so listen up." Then, in great detail, he acquainted them with the area around the Institute, the buildings, the streets, the nearest police and fire stations and the routine and times when the students would be going to and from classes at the University.

"Now, here are the prints of the building. You will notice it has one door leading from the roof to a stairwell and, according to the drawings, the door can only be opened from the inside. You men will lead the assault on the building and I'll send another eight of our boys from the east side to help you."

"How we going in?" Billy Frazier asked.

"I'm getting to that. There's a chopper rental company in Skokie and I have men who can fly them. You'll meet in Skokie, board the choppers and fly down to the Institute, then rappel from the choppers to the roof."

He also explained there would be a diversion he believed would help them accomplish their mission.

"We've hired a torch to set fire to a couple of buildings at the University and that should tie up traffic and draw attention away from what's going down at the Institute."

"Luka, will there be guards on the roof?" Joey Falco asked.

"Probably, so you'll need to carry your high-powered rifles and take out the guards before you rappel down to the roof. Then you'll blow the door with C-4 and enter the building from the roof, try to neutralize any muscle you encounter and nab Casstevens and the broad who is with him."

"When do we jump off and what about weapons?" Ramon Chavez asked.

"You must be in Skokie at 7 o'clock tomorrow morning to pick up the choppers so you'll need to fly into Chicago tonight."

He opened a gun case that was on the table. "We've brought in some of these H & K automatic weapons with silencers."

"So what happens after we nab the doctor?" Bailey Buchanan asked.

"Yeah, good question, Bailey. After you nab the doctor and the broad, the chopper pilots will lower cables and harness and wench you all up. You will return to Meigs field where our jet will be waiting to bring the doctor back to New York."

"How are we going to know if he is in the building?" Frazier asked.

"I'll contact you on your cell phone with that information so you will instruct the pilots to circle high above the building until you hear from me. Any questions?"

There were none.

CHAPTER TWENTY-FOUR

D'Angelo awakened Alexander Culverwell at 6 a.m. and helped him into the hot tub for his morning bath then assisted him with getting dressed.

"Frankie, this is a great day and the future is bright," Culverwell said as his friend shaved his face and trimmed his mustache. "I have hope for the first time in years."

"Yes, Mr. C, and I'm glad I can share it with you. You've always been very generous with me and I'll never forget it. You are deserving of this good fortune."

"You know, Frankie, if you ever lose your dream, life is over."

A few minutes later Bruiser Brown pushed the breakfast cart into the bedroom.

"Good morning, Mr. C, juice and toast and a full pot of coffee."

"Just some coffee."

"You need to eat, Mr. C, to keep your strength up."

"Bruiser, there'll be time a plenty for eating later."

Culverwell sipped on the coffee. "Bruiser, please tell Dr. Casstevens that we will meet in the conference room at 8 a.m."

"Yes Sir, I'll tell him immediately."

Bruiser Brown knocked on V. J.'s door. "Dr. Casstevens, Mr. Culverwell will meet with you and 8 a.m."

"Yes, of course." V. J. informed Macee of the meeting. "I don't know how long it will last."

V. J. arrived at the penthouse sitting room at exactly 8 a.m. and minutes later Culverwell entered the room.

"We meet once again, Dr. Casstevens and I trust you had a good night's rest?"

"Yes, thank you."

"I never really rest much, but even a couple of hours renews my strength and helps me face the new day."

Sitting there looking at the old man, V. J. realized that for some the golden years are not really so golden and life is filled with certain agonies before the end comes and a man takes that very long goodbye.

"Doctor, I believe our meeting here, even under these somewhat strained circumstances, will prove to be quite rewarding for both of us."

"Again, I question whether I have anything to offer." V. J. knew he must find a way to survive in this old man's world, a world far away from the fun and frolic in the French Quarter, a world he knew nothing about.

Culverwell gasped for air with a heaving chest. "You know, Doctor, some people carry destiny around in their pocket, and I believe you are one of those people."

"You may be vastly overestimating my gifts and abilities."

"I have amassed one of the great fortunes in this land but who I am and what I possess is of no particular consequence for I am a dying man." Culverwell's eyes blinked incessantly behind steel-rimmed glasses. "If you want to find the pot of gold at the end of the rainbow then you need to bring your own gold and I have enough to make you a very rich man, like a multi-millionaire."

V. J. pondered what the old man said. *Just a few days*

ago Doctor Townsend threatened to cut off my seventy-five grand a year and I thought how distasteful it would be working for wages. Look at me now, a wealthy old man is offering me great wealth to give him a few more years of life.

"That's very generous of you, Mr. Culverwell, but I hope we have not had a major misunderstanding."

"What do you mean?"

"You undoubtedly believe I have made a major breakthrough with my experiments with the chimpanzee, experiments that could be of benefit to you but there are so many unknown factors in my research."

"I am convinced that your research is credible and will stand up under scientific scrutiny. I want to be the subject of your next experiment and I have the faith to believe that you will be able to put the dreadful days of my past to sleep forever."

"But there are so many questions still to be answered. Was my experiment successful on the chimpanzee because of the animal's unique DNA? If so, it might not work for you or me. Was it just a one-time chance kind of thing with the chimp that might not even work on other animals?"

"Most men crave the chance to be their own masters, however questionable that mastery might be in light of the actions they take. I'm willing to take that chance and be delivered once and for all from days filled with silence and nights that never end."

V. J. felt a sudden and chilling premonition and it worried him. *This old man has designs far beyond the ability of science to reverse his age and make him strong again. Right now his demeanor is benign and lyrical. But what about tomorrow?*

"Doctor, our generation with all its accomplisments will be known as the fallen generation because of so many wars, disasters and poverty. It is the most humili-ating century in history. Man is the king of the earth but also his own worst enemy. Yet there are universal har-monies hidden beneath the chaotic experiences of our lives."

"I'm confident that you and I are in complete agree-ment that man is his own worst enemy. But even that fallen generation has accomplished some good: penicil-lin, the polio vaccine and a thousand other cures." *Am I talking to a genius or just an old man with a depraved mind? I don't think he can distinguish between sun and shadow.*

"I wince at the inescapable certainty of approaching death and before that last door slams, I want another chance at life. Sometimes I feel like I have just stepped over the threshold and life is already gone and infirmi-ty, like a shadow, is always by my side like a nightmare that whispers in the dark. Were I to be reborn, it would be like having one foot in heaven before the devil knows I'm gone."

V. J. sensed the old man's inner demons had threat-ened his loss of reason.

"Doctor, we are getting nowhere. I thought you would be more cooperative and we could work togeth-er to bring about a great transformation in our world. We must reach a consensus. What can I do to convince you that we can work together?"

He rang the bell and Bruiser Brown entered the room and handed him several pills and a glass of water. V. J. noticed he was tired and haggard.

The old man's hands trembled as he took the pills and V. J. noticed a far-away look of mystery in his eyes.

"Now, Doctor, let's get down to business. I'm pre-pared to pay you millions of dollars, whatever you ask, to give my life back to me." His tone was dictatorial, perhaps a reaction to rage too long suppressed.

"I don't know if that is possible," V. J. said as he tried to cushion the old man's emotions away from too much finality.

"Do you have any idea how the world will be changed if you can perfect your scientific discovery and make it available on some broad scale? With your knowledge of science and my knowledge of the business world we can create unbelievable wealth, the kind of wealth that no human being could even imagine. And we can bring peace to all mankind. Yes, we are looking at the hinges of history and we must fulfill our sacred calling."

"It sounds genuinely humanitarian but is it possible? I'm not prepared to give you a conclusive answer at this point in my research." *At least he's starting to be open and honest with his intentions. He wants to use the discovery to give his life back to him but also for his own fanatical dreams.*

"Doctor, we could rule the world! Can't you see that you could provide the tools for a great scientific renaissance where certain people could live a hundred fifty, two hundred years and the world would reap the benefits of their ageless wisdom?"

V. J. listened intently but said nothing. *He is treading softly through an ethical minefield. But he's beginning to show his true colors. He's a Promethian-faith progressive who wants to make gods out of devils.*

"Even as we speak this day we could be on the verge of a wonderful new civilization where we could defeat sickness and disease and return this world to a Garden of Eden, a Shangri La."

V. J. frowned, a studied look of concern on his face. "Even if we were to determine this discovery can be translated into improving the health of thousands, maybe even millions of people, how would we use it? Who would receive it, and who would be denied? We are no gods, no arbiters of life and death; we are mere humans with all the frailties common to man. And I have no intention of setting deadlines for any man's immortality or his extinction."

"You miss the point. I will show you how to make that determination. The only rule will be that there are no rules. First, we will profile all the great leaders of the world: scientists, economists, educators, successful businessmen and make sure their lives are preserved. Second, we will protect the lives of athletes in order to create a stronger, healthier race of people here on earth. Third, we will provide the treatment to artists, writers, great musicians, and the creative people who will be able to make all of our lives more enjoyable. Finally, we will set up tests to determine the IQ of certain people and if they qualify, their lives will be preserved."

"What about all the others? What would become of the sick and infirmed, the elderly, the handicapped, the criminals in our prisons and the patients in our mental institutions?" Suddenly V. J. realized that the human heart is capable of the worst of evil when that heart is cut off from the law of nature and nature's God.

Culverwell pondered the question and scratched his head. "Perhaps with some exceptions, these people would be allowed to live out their natural lives but would not benefit from life extension."

The old man paused as though in deep thought. "Of course you realize that unless we learn how to reduce and then control the world's population in the next few years we will destroy ourselves. I think it is commonly understood that there are too many people on this planet and the numbers must be reduced for the common good of all the rest of us. Otherwise we will be on the wrong side of history."

"It sounds as though you already have a master plan for the future of the world. But your plan would only benefit the wealthy and gifted but do nothing for all the other people."

The old man's countenance turned cold and sinister."We have no obligation to our post-mortem days but only to our present generation. Do we understand one another and are you ready to proceed with the treatment?"

"I do understand, but I don't want to have anything to do with you or your vision of the future of mankind and, even if I choose to cooperate, I will need more time for research."

"No, unequivocally no! I'm asking you if you are willing to cooperate with me now? We don't have time!" he screamed.

When D'Angelo and Bruiser Brown heard him, they rushed into the room.

"You okay, Mr. C?" D'Angelo asked.

He did not reply.

"Doctor, I have established the Culverwell Scientific Research Institute near the University of Chicago. We have a state-of-the-art laboratory there and I will ask my associates to escort you there for your orientation."

"I might like to see the lab, but I'm not going to perform any other tests and don't care to pursue this discussion any further."

"I spent millions of dollars on the Institute and there is no finer in the world. Any scientist in America worth his salt would be honored to work in such a place."

"I'm just not any scientist." V. J. realized he was

now seeing the soft underbelly of the beast.

"That is totally unacceptable!" Culverwell yelled as his face lost all its color. "I bring you here and offer you the world, riches and power and fame, and you are not interested."

Culverwell motioned to D'Angelo to bend down so he could whisper something to him. "Frankie, bring in the girl, we're going to find out right now how serious Dr. Casstevens is in his intransigent position."

"Yes, Mr. C."

D'Angelo left the room and in a few minutes returned with Macee.

"V. J., what you all doing?" Macee asked.

"It's okay, Macee."

"Now, Doctor, this is a pivotal moment in history," Culverwell said. "You can either choose to cooperate with me or lose your girlfriend."

"What do you mean?"

"Show him, Frankie."

D'Angelo nodded to Bruiser Brown who opened the large sliding glass door that led out to a sun deck. The two men grabbed Macee's arms and pulled her out to the deck. She screamed when Bruiser Brown threw her over his shoulder and the two men held her by the ankles and dangled her over the side of the building.

Macee screamed and yelled. "Help, somebody help me, please somebody!"

V. J. glared at the old man then lunged across the room and reached down and grabbed Macee by the leg and tried to pull her back up onto the deck.

Bruiser Brown hit him in the jaw with his fist and knocked him to the floor as Macee continued to thrash back and forth and scream for help.

"Now, Doctor, either you pledge your cooperation

or your girlfriend goes over the side and I'll remind you it's fifty floors to the ground."

"Okay, yeah I'll work with you, just don't harm Macee."

"Bring her up, boys," Culverwell said as D'Angelo and Bruiser Brown raised her up and led her back inside the penthouse and closed the sliding glass doors.

Macee was trembling and pale as a ghost as V. J. put his arms around her and held her close to him. "Are you okay, Macee?"

Bruiser Brown led her back to her room where she fell onto the bed and covered her head with a blanket.

Visions of Macee dangling over the side of the building haunted V. J. and made him want to throw up. At that point he realized that Macee was a lot more to him than just a good friend.

"Now, Doctor, you will be ready to depart for the Institute at ten o'clock this morning. Frankie will escort you and I trust you will be prepared to perform the treatment on me quite soon."

V. J. was trembling and Culverwell could see that his nerves were shot.

"I'll be ready and I will need Ms. Marineaux and Rufus the chimpanzee there with me."

"Oh, why is that?"

"I want to do some blood work on the chimpanzee for further analysis of his condition and Ms. Marineaux will act as my lab assistant."

"Yes, of course."

V. J. stood to leave.

"There's one other thing, Doctor, please don't think you could deceive me for I will have trained scientists monitoring every move you make. And you know that it would be futile trying to escape from my people for we found you once and we would find you again. Do we have an understanding?"

"Yes, I believe we do."

V. J. went to Macee's room and found her in bed with the covers pulled up over her head. He sat down on the bed and pulled back the covers. "Macee, how you doing?"

"Okay, I guess. I was thinking about you and how nice it would be to get a great big hug and kiss."

He smiled, leaned over the bed and wrapped his arms around her, then kissed her on the forehead.

"I've got some lips, you know."

"Yeah, I know," he said, then kissed her again on the lips.

"Macee you're wonderful and I'm proud to have you as a friend."

"Is that all we are, just friends?"

"No, you're my very special friend."

"Hmm, very special friend, I like the sound of that."

"I'm sorry about everything that has happened to you, but you are a winner."

"I just about got thrown off the top of a big building and I'm a little shaky but I think I'm going to be all right."

"That's good."

"What's going to become of us? Are we going to die?"

"No, we're not going to die."

"Did you know that women live longer than men?"

"So?"

"Just thought I would throw that in."

"This morning we're going to the Institute down near the University to run some tests on Rufus to determine if this reversal he has experienced is permanent. Then, Culverwell wants me to give him a treatment but I promise you that will never happen."

"V. J., you're so smart and I'm proud of you."

"Thanks and I'm proud of you."

D'Angelo knocked on the door to V. J.'s room. "We'll be leaving in twenty minutes."

When D'Angelo returned, V. J. and Macee were waiting in the penthouse lounge.

"What you going to do with the chimp?" D'Angelo asked.

"I plan to take him with us and perform some tests."

"I don't know, maybe we ought to lock him up in the closet and leave him here."

"Mr. Culverwell has already given his approval."

"I'll check it out."

At the appointed time D'Angelo and Bruiser Brown accompanied V. J., Macee and the chimp down to the first floor and to the waiting limousine.

They arrived at the Institute thirty minutes later and the driver parked right in front of the building. Bruiser Brown opened the door and motioned for V. J. and Macee to follow him.

Dula fixed his binoculars on the limousine and yelled "Domino" when he saw V. J., Macee and Rufus as they walked toward the entrance to the Institute.

"Banion, loan me your cell phone, I need to call the Chief."

The detective handed him the phone and he dialed New Orleans PD.

"Chief Landry's office," the secretary said.

"This is Dula, let me talk to the Chief."

"Scott, what's going on?" Chief Landry asked.

"We've had this place staked out all night and the hunch paid off. Casstevens and his woman showed up at the Culverwell Institute about five minutes ago and we're going to ask Captain O'Reilly to send in a SWAT team to rescue them."

"Good work, Scott, and can I tell the mayor and council that we finally have a break in the case?"

"Yeah, it's a big break."

"Okay, you and Charlie bring the doctor back to New Orleans."

"Ten-four."

Dula asked Banion to call Captain O'Reilly and request a SWAT team.

Healy John Hurt met D'Angelo and Bruiser Brown at the front entrance and escorted V. J. and Macee to the elevator. Bruiser then returned to the Culverwell Building penthouse to help the old man get ready for a trip to the Institute for the treatment.

The elevator door opened on the fifth floor. V. J.'s mouth dropped open. He had never seen such a magnificent laboratory and research facility. There were state-of-the-art inverted microscope image splitters that transmit images from the microscope into nearby cameras; Optical Doppler Velocemeters to increase the movement of red blood cells; a fluorescence detection camera which transfers images to a computer that prints out the information; and a large freezer unit for preserving blood and other research specimens. V. J. also saw a Computerized Axial Tomography scanner in a side room and an MRI in another. And there were computer stations, located strategically throughout the lab, and an infirmary.

"Dr. V. J. Casstevens, I want you to meet Dr. Walker Bannister, the director of the Culverwell Institute," D'Angelo said.

The two men shook hands. V. J. wondered why a distinguished-looking man like Bannister was working for Culverwell.

"Welcome to the Culverwell Institute, Dr. Casstevens, we've been anxiously awaiting your arrival."

"Thank you, Doctor, and this is my friend Macee Marineaux."

"It's my pleasure, Ms. Marineaux. And this must be the chimpanzee we've heard so much about."

Someone has really done their homework. I guess these men have seen the clandestine videos of my lab work in New Orleans.

"Dr. Bannister, I'm sure you will want to show the doctor and Ms. Marineaux around the lab and if you will excuse me, I have a couple of matters to attend to," D'Angelo said.

"Yes, Doctor, Ms. Marineaux, please come into my office and be seated, I also have a matter that needs attention so if you will excuse me."

Dr. Bannister left the office. V. J. turned to Macee. "There's something I've wanted to tell you."

"Oh?"

"Macee, I think you're wonderful."

"What a nice thing to say."

"And I've been doing a lot of thinking."

"Yes?"

"We're together all the time anyway," V. J. said, almost embarrassed, "and I never would want to be away from you, so if it's okay I want you be my wife someday, like when this is all over."

"Oh, yes, yes, yes and does that mean that you love me?"

"Kinda sort of, I guess."

"No, V. J., I'm not ever going to be your wife unless

you *really* love me. I've tried that three times already."

"Okay, I really love you."

"And I love you too, V. J., and actually I've loved you for two years but didn't feel like you cared anything at all about me."

"Well I don't like rushing into anything."

"I don't think two years is rushing things."

"I know."

"What did it take to make up your mind?"

"Macee, when those men held you over the side of the building, I couldn't stand the thought of losing you and it was then I realized how much you really mean to me."

"Oh, V. J., that makes me the happiest woman in the world."

V. J. smiled and hugged her.

CHAPTER TWENTY-FIVE

Police Captain Blaine called Avanzini from New Orleans and informed him that Dr. Casstevens had arrived at the Culverwell Institute.

"Thank you, Captain, you have been a big help to us and we'll have another letter in the mail to you today. We always like to take good care of our friends."

"We'll continue to monitor the Chief's calls."

"Yes, that would be good."

Luka contacted Billy Frazier in one of the helicopters circling high above the Institute and told him the subject was in the building. "Move in and take Dr. Casstevens."

"We're on our way."

Frazier tapped the pilot on the shoulder and pointed down and the helicopters began their descent. He asked the pilot to bank the craft so his men could get a clear shot at the two armed guards on the roof. They leaned out the side door of the helicopter and fired several rounds, killing both of them.

The pilots dropped down to within fifty feet of the roof as all the men, dressed in black and wearing ski masks, rappelled down to the roof of the building.

Frazier removed a handful of C-4 plastic explosives from a bag, carefully filled the crack of the door to the stairwell and stepped back to protect himself from the explosion.

Dula heard the explosion and two other explosions

and spotted two fires on the university campus. Within minutes a half-dozen fire trucks, their shrill sirens blaring, raced down the street trying to weave their way through the thousands of students, yelling and screaming as a general panic swept the campus, ran out into the streets, blocking traffic.

"Charlie, did you hear that?"

"I heard three explosions."

"Yeah, but one of them came from the Institute."

The three detectives jumped out of the car and ran toward the building but the front door was locked. Dula pulled out his automatic and fired three rounds into the lock, then kicked the door open.

They rushed to the elevator but discovered that it had been disabled.

"Let's try the stairs!" Dula shouted. However, the heavy steel door to the stairwell apparently was bolted from the inside and he could not open it.

The brown van carrying the SWAT team entered Plaisance Street and the driver blew his horn but the frightened students continued running across the street blocking traffic.

After blowing the door, Frazier and his men ran down the stairwell to the fifth floor where they saw two of Culverwell's men standing guard at the entrance to the lab. Frazier fired his automatic weapon and killed them both. Then he and his men slowly entered the lab.

D'Angelo heard the shots. "Healy, check that out and see what's going on!"

Healy reached the door where he encountered the armed men in black. He keyed his radio. "We got visitors!"

"How many are they?" D'Angelo asked.

"I see a dozen!"

Healy pulled out his Beretta Nine Millimeter automatic and began firing at the men in black. They returned the fire and kept Healy dodging bullets while one of the men crawled on his stomach down the hallway to the door, raised up and shot Healy twice in the chest. He dropped to the floor.

"Everyone get down! Now!" D'Angelo yelled.

He pulled a twelve-gauge shotgun from a case and began firing at the men in black, killing two of them and wounding another as they rushed through the door.

V. J. pulled both Macee and Rufus down to the floor and covered them with his body as the screaming scientists and lab technicians scrambled for cover.

Frazier lobbed a smoke grenade at D'Angelo and, with his survival knife between his teeth and firing his automatic weapon, moved through the smoke toward where he was hiding.

Blinded by the smoke, D'Angelo fired the shotgun at random at any sound he heard. Frazier came up behind him and shoved the knife between his ribs, killing him instantly.

D'Angelo's other men reached the fifth floor and ran down the hallway toward the lab. The men in black caught them in a cross fire and killed three of them then engaged the others in hand-to-hand combat. Within minutes all of D'Angelo's men and three men in black were dead.

Rufus crawled out from under V. J. and ran into the lab. The hair was bristling on the back of his neck and his lips tightened in a ferocious scowl as he began throwing books at the intruders. Frazier fired three shots at the chimp and he dropped to the floor.

When V. J. saw that Rufus had been shot, he charged

out of the director's office, dodging bullets, and picked up Rufus and held him in his arms. Rufus licked his face, grunted ever so quietly and died.

V. J. laid Rufus's lifeless body down on the floor.

"You shouldn't have killed Rufus, he never ever bothered anybody!"

He kicked in the glass cover over the fire alarm and it shattered. Then he took out the fire axe and charged Frazier who was so surprised he raised his arm to protect himself then hit V. J. in the head with the butt of his automatic weapon knocking him to the floor.

The smoke cleared as the scientists and their aides walked around the room in a daze, speaking in hushed tones and trying to find out what had happened.

V. J. reached up and felt the blood on the wound on his head. Macee saw he was hurt and went to the bathroom and dampened a cloth.

She returned to the lab and wiped the blood away. "It's a bad cut but it'll be okay."

She went over to Rufus's lifeless body, picked him up and held him in her arms. "You were my friend and better than most people I know." She laid him back down.

"Okay, men, let's get out of here!" Frazier yelled.

He looked down at V. J. "Dr. Casstevens, you'll be coming with us and we must hurry."

"Where are we going?"

"I'll tell you later."

They made their way to the roof. V. J. saw several steel cables coming down from one of the helicopters with belts and straps dangling from the ends. Frazier strapped the belts around V. J. and Macee and signaled for the pilot to hoist them up. The other pilots lowered the cables to lift up the men in black who had survived the battle. When they were all aboard, the pilots banked the helicopters and headed toward Meigs Field.

The SWAT team finally made it to the Institute, used explosives to knock down the door to the stairwell and ran up the stairs, followed by Dula, Francis and Banion.

They found bodies scattered all along the hallway and inside the lab. Dula hurried up on the roof just as the helicopters disappeared beyond the campus.

"Banion, you got radio contact with Air Eagle Ten?" Dula asked.

"Yeah, I think so."

"Could you call him for me?"

"Yeah, Air Eagle Ten this is car forty-eight, you copy?"

"Go ahead car forty-eight."

"Lieutenant Dula from New Orleans wants to talk to you."

"Go ahead."

"Air Eagle Ten, what's your twenty?"

"Monitoring the fires at the University."

"Two choppers just left the area of the Culverwell Institute near the campus, did you see them?"

"Yeah, I thought they were a couple of TV choppers covering the fires."

"The guys in the choppers just kidnapped Dr. V. J. Casstevens, a well-known New Orleans scientist. Can you tail them for me and let me know where they go?"

"Ten-four, I'm on my way."

Ten minutes later the Air Eagle Ten pilot reported to Dula. "One of the choppers landed at Meigs Field. Three of the passengers on the chopper transferred to a Lear Jet that was standing by. The other chopper broke and flew north along Lake Michigan."

"Thanks, Air Eagle Ten."

Dula turned to Banion. "Can you get us to Meigs Field?"

They hurried downstairs and out into the street to the unmarked police car. Banion attached his flashing light to the top of the car.

They arrived at Meigs Field thirty minutes later and drove up to the office.

Banion pushed it open. "Chicago PD."

"Yeah, yeah, okay, I'm cool," the manager said.

"You had a Lear fly out of here about a half hour ago, where was it headed?" Dula asked.

"They filed a flight plan for MacArthur Airport up on Long Island."

"And you're sure about that?"

"Yeah."

"Did you get the Lear's ID?"

"It's right here on the bill, and they paid by cash."

They returned to the squad car. Dula asked Banion to let him use his cell phone again. He keyed the phone for New York directory assistance and asked for Michael Murphy O'Leary who had served with him in Vietnam.

When the operator gave him the number, he dialed O'Leary's residence.

"Go ahead, this is Mike."

"Mike, this is a voice out of the past."

"Yeah, I know who it is, how you doing Sarge? I thought they had all the outlaws in jail."

"Well, I'm trying to stay on the straight and narrow."

"What's going on, Sarge?"

"Mike, I need your help."

"Name it."

"Any of the old gang from the First Marines still

around?"

"Yeah, one or two."

"If you can, call a couple of them and tell them I need some help."

"Okay, what you got."

"I'm tailing some kidnappers who left Chicago by private jet about thirty minutes ago bound for MacArthur Airport up on Long Island just off of Interstate 495 between Holbrook and Bohemia. Think you and some of the boys could get up there and check it out for me?"

"What time will it arrive?"

"Sometime around 1 p.m."

"It will take a while to round up the boys, but sure, Sarge, we'll get on up there, and what we looking for?"

"There should be a man and a woman being held hostage and they will be transferred to ground transportation after they land. I want you to follow them, and don't lose them."

"We're on our way, Sarge."

"By the way, you got a cell phone?"

"Yeah, number 212 773-5555."

"Okay, get crackin, and I'll buy you boys a beer."

Dula turned to the office manager. "We need a jet."

"Where you going?"

"New York City, LaGuardia."

"Look, it's none of my business, but can you boys afford a thousand bucks an hour?"

Banion bristled. "This is a police matter and Chicago PD will stand good for it."

"Okay, I'll have to get a pilot out here and it'll take some time to get the plane ready."

Dula and Francis thanked Banion for all his help and said goodbye.

"Let's do it again, sometime," Banion said.

Dula grinned. "Not in this lifetime."

"By the way, you take my cell phone, you may need it."

"Thanks Jack and if you're ever looking for another job come see me and Charlie in New Orleans."

"Maybe someday."

The pilot lifted off from Meigs Field at exactly 1 p.m. and headed for New York LaGuardia.

CHAPTER TWENTY-SIX

Michael Murphy O'Leary and two of his old Marine buddies, Tank McMillan and Carter Rogers, arrived at the MacArthur Airport on Long Island and drove into the parking lot where they could get a clear view of all incoming flights.

The Lear Jet landed thirty minutes later and taxied up to a private hangar.

The pilot opened the side door, lowered the stairs and Frazier escorted V. J. and Macee down to the tarmac and on to the waiting limousine where three of Luka Avanzini's men met them.

The driver of the limousine pulled out of the airport and headed toward Interstate 495 and then west toward the city. O'Leary and his friends followed from a safe distance, undetected.

When they reached Lower Manhattan, the driver headed toward Chinatown and pulled up in front of the House of Fong Imports and Exports Emporium where he parked the limousine. He opened the back door. O'Leary saw a man and woman get out and follow three men into the building. Minutes later they returned to their waiting limousine and drove away.

"Guess we better hang out here until we hear from the sarge," O'Leary told McMillan and Rogers.

When their jet landed at LaGuardia, Dula and Francis thanked the pilot then headed toward the main terminal. Dula keyed his cell phone and called O'Leary.

"Yeah, this is Mike."

"Mike, what you got?"

"I don't know for sure, but we tailed the man and woman to a place down in Chinatown called the House of Fong Imports and Exports on Chambers Street. They arrived in a limousine and we've been watching the place but haven't seen any movement in the last hour."

"Okay, Mike, we'll catch a taxi and head on down there, should take about forty-five minutes."

"Good show, Sarge, we'll be waiting for you."

"And Mike, thanks, and thank the boys for me."

"You bet."

Wu-tang Fong and several Chinese agents who flew in from Washington, D. C., bowed to V. J. and Macee. "Welcome to the House of Fong, you are my honored guests," Fong said.

"Do you mind telling us what we're doing here?" V. J. asked.

"Not at all, you are the guests of the Peoples Republic of China and you soon will be on your way to Beijing where you will be able to continue your very dramatic scientific research."

V. J. wondered if the nightmare would ever end. *Maybe a guy ought to pinch himself to make sure he isn't dreaming. Now the Chinese enter the equation. How could this be happening to us?*

Macee held V. J.'s trembling hand. "Do you think we could see the Great Wall of China while we're there? I always wanted to see it since I read about it in high school."

"Yeah, Macee, we can see the wall."

Wu-tang Fong planned to keep the twenty-million

dollars he promised Luka Avanzini and was quite proud of his charade. *Only the inscrutable Oriental mind could conceive such a plan and it will make me a very rich man. I will keep the twenty-million and Luka Avanzini's aging father will never receive the treatment from Dr. Casstevens that I promised him – and I am glad. Let the old man go ahead and die. The young punk Luka is going to be surprised when he arrives at the House of Fong tomorrow morning – no money, no Dr. Casstevens.*

But he knew it would be necessary for him to return to China for no one could double-cross Luka Avanzini and live.

Wu-tang Fong smiled as he contemplated the fate of Dr. Casstevens and his girlfriend. The Chinese Ambassador in Washington had informed him that his government was not remotely interested in the Doctor's discovery, that Beijing actually wanted him eliminated.

"We already have too many people in China and Dr. Casstevens' work, if it is credible, would only increase our severe population problems," the ambassador had told him. "The chairman himself has issued the order to get rid of him so that no other country can benefit from his research. That is the official position from Beijing."

"Now, it's my duty to eliminate Dr. Casstevens and his woman and that should be relatively easy," Wu-tang Fong informed the ambassador. "I will arrange passage for them on a container ship on which our operatives will have placed a powerful bomb. The bomb will destroy the ship soon after it leaves New York Harbor."

Wu-tang Fong returned to his office where his men were holding V. J. and Macee.

"What's your timetable for our departure for China?" V. J. asked.

"You will leave at four o'clock this afternoon on the

Kyushu Maru, a Japanese freighter sailing for the Panama Canal then on to Shanghai. It will be necessary for you and your woman to be temporarily sedated and then you will be placed in the false bottom of a large shipping crate to elude the customs agents. After the ship clears the harbor, the captain will release you and you will become passengers and receive the very best of everything the ship has to offer."

"Is he saying we've got to be put to sleep?" Macee asked.

"Yeah, I think so."

"Well, I don't like that idea at all."

"Ms. Marineaux, the sedative will last only a few hours, then you will wake up and enjoy a wonderful voyage with all expenses paid."

"I don't think I'm going."

"I'm so sorry, but you have no choice."

Wu-tang Fong motioned to his agents to subdue V.J. and Macee and tie their hands behind them. Then one of the agents removed two syringes from a black bag.

When Macee began to yell and scream and kick, Wu-tang Fong ordered his men to gag her. Then the agent with the syringe injected her in her left arm.

Within seconds the sedative took effect and Macee leaned over against V. J. and went sound asleep. Then the agent injected him.

They moved them to a large wooden crate with a false bottom then filled the remainder of the crate with a variety of exports bound for Shanghai.

Wu-tang Fong picked up the phone and called the ACE Delivery Service. "We have a shipment for the *Kyushu Maru* on Pier 58 and we want it loaded before the ship sails at four o'clock. I have already cleared all the paperwork with Captain Takeda so he will be ready to load the crate as soon as you arrive at the pier."

Dula and Francis found O'Leary's car near the Emporium and climbed inside where Dula greeted his old buddies from Vietnam.

"Hey Tank, Carter, Mike, this is my partner Detective Charlie Francis from New Orleans. And Charlie, this is one bad bunch of Marines and I ought to know, I had to baby sit them for three years in Nam."

"Well, Sarge, seems like we pulled you out of a couple of scrapes in Da Nang," O'Leary said. "Remember the night you got into the fight with the four sailors?"

"Yeah, I thought I was holding my own."

"You sure were, all four of them were on top of you," Tank McMillan said, laughing.

"Now Sarge, what's this all about?" O'Leary asked.

"Mike, it's a long story but we had this scientist working in a research center in New Orleans and some people say he has made a very important scientific discovery. Then some bad boys from Chicago kidnapped him and his girlfriend and there was a big shootout with some New York boys."

"So the New York boys must have won because the Doctor wound up here," O'Leary said. "So what's the plan and how can we help you?"

"We're going to play it by ear."

An hour later a large truck pulled up in front of the House of Fong and picked up several crates.

V. J. watched the truck drive away. "This guy Fong has plenty of business."

At exactly 4 p.m., Dula saw ten people leave the House of Fong and he presumed they were employees. *I wonder what's going on inside. I'm tired of waiting. Just sitting here doing nothing gives me the willies.*

He decided to make his move. "Boys, let's do it. Charlie and I will go in the front and Mike you and the boys cover the back."

"You got any weapons?" Francis asked.

"Yeah, a couple of shotguns in the trunk," O'Leary replied.

"Okay, let's rock and roll," Dula said as they slid out of the car and walked toward the House of Fong. They made their way up to the front door. V. J. slowly opened the door, stepped inside and could hear voices coming from a back room.

The detectives crouched down low and made their way toward the room, past all kinds of lamps, statues and ornaments including a fat Buddha, as the voices became louder. Dula frowned and shook his head when he realized they were speaking Chinese.

V. J. raised up, looked through a window and saw six men in the room talking animatedly, flailing the air, laughing and toasting one another. He saw a couple of Uzis on a desk and a rifle standing against a file cabinet. He presumed the men were also carrying side arms.

Dula crawled over to where Francis was hiding. "Charlie, go around back and tell the boys what we've got and that we're going in."

"Scott, you don't think this is a loser's play?"

"No, we've got the element of surprise. Tell the boys to hit the back door at exactly 5:15 p.m. So set your watch with theirs."

"Okay, Scott, I'll be right back."

Francis made his way to the door and ran to the back of the store.

"Mike, we've got six heavily armed men in there," Francis said. "We're going in at 5:15 so let's synchronize our watches, we can't afford any mistakes with these guys."

Francis returned to the front and worked his way toward the office in the back of the store. Then he gave a thumbs-up to Dula.

At exactly 5:15 they charged into the office. "Police, everybody down on the floor!"

One of the Chinese agents grabbed an Uzi but Dula shot him in the chest before he could fire the weapon. Two other agents ran for the back door but O'Leary and his men surprised them, hit them with the butts of the shotguns and laid them out on the floor. The others held up their hands and surrendered.

When things settled down, Dula asked, "Now, who's in charge here?"

"I am Wu-tang Fong of the House of Fong, and officer we have violated no laws of any kind."

"Now Mr. Fong, we know that you brought a man and a woman in here a couple of hours ago and I don't see them around anywhere. Mind telling me what became of them?"

"I don't know what you are talking about."

Dula pulled his Beretta out of the holster and slowly screwed on a silencer. "Mr. Fong, I'm going to ask you one more time, where are they?"

"So sorry, but I told you I don't know."

Dula fired one shot at his kneecap and Wu-tang Fong yelled and winced in pain.

"Now, Mr. Fong, before I shoot your other knee and you never walk again, do you want to tell me where the man and woman are?"

"Yes, just don't shoot me. They are aboard the Japanese container ship *Kyushu Maru* and they left Pier 58 more than an hour ago."

"Okay, Mr. Fong, we're going after the them but if you're lying to me, I'll be back and take you out permanently."

"No, you are too late, our agents placed a bomb on the ship and it will explode at 6:30 p.m. and completely destroy the ship. You will never be able to rescue them in time."

"But we can try."

Dula took his cell phone out of his pocket and dialed Chief Landry's office in New Orleans.

The secretary put him through to the Chief. "Scott, speak to me!"

"We're in big trouble and need your help."

"Go on."

"Dr. Casstevens and Ms. Marineaux have sailed out of New York Harbor on a ship by the name of *Kyushu Maru* and there is a bomb on board set to go off in about an hour. We need you to get in touch with Commissioner Kelly of the NYPD and ask him to send a chopper down here in Chinatown in the next fifteen minutes. We might have a chance to rescue them."

"I'll give it a shot and I sure hope I can locate Commissioner Kelly."

"Go for it, boss, and tell Kelly there is a vacant lot about a block north of the House of Fong Emporium. We'll meet the chopper there."

"Okay, Scott."

Dula and Francis handed their cuffs to O'Leary. "Cuff 'em, Mike, then call the FBI and tell them to come and pick up these bad boys," Dula said.

"Yeah, Sarge."

"And after the feds get here, tell them Mr. Fong will need some medical attention. He fell and hurt himself."

O'Leary grinned.

Before they left the Emporium, Dula saw two large briefcases on a footlocker beside the desk and, curious, opened one of them. A grin creased his face when he saw the contents. "Look here, Charlie, there must be two million dollars in here, all hundred-dollar bills. When he opened the second briefcase he saw that it, too, was filled with stacks of hundred dollar bills.

"Wonder what's in the footlocker?" Francis asked.

Dula fired two shots at the lock and opened the lid. "Charlie, we've hit the mother lode."

"What do you mean?"

Charlie saw dozens of stacks of hundred-dollar bills. "Who said crime doesn't pay?"

Dula looked down at Wu-tang Fong. "What were you going to do with all this money? Would I be correct if I were to assume that you stole if from someone? Maybe the mob?"

"Yes, and I would do it again."

Dula carried the briefcases with him as they left the Emporium. Charlie and one of the other men carried the footlocker and placed it in the trunk of O'Leary's car.

"Okay, Charlie let's go over to the vacant lot."

"Yeah, and hope the chopper gets here in time."

"I know it's a long shot."

"Yeah, but maybe we'll get a break."

"I hope Dr. Casstevens' luck hasn't run out."

"Yeah, buddy."

The next fifteen minutes seemed like an eternity. Scott wondered if the police helicopter would show up or if the chase was over and they had lost.

Francis was the first to hear the rat-tat-tat of the rotors as the helicopter appeared overhead and the pilot set the craft down in the vacant lot. Dula made the sign of the cross over his chest. "Thank you, Lord."

"You a Christian?" Francis asked.

"No, I'm not even religious but I may be after this thing is over."

"Both of us."

The detectives crouched down to avoid the rotor blades and climbed aboard the craft.

"Thanks for helping us out," Dula told the pilot.

"No sweat, Lieutenant, I'm Russ and this is Detective Art Sinclair of the 12th Precinct," Russ Hodges, the pilot said. "The Commissioner asked Art to come along in case you need some help."

"Thanks, men, and this is what we've got and it ain't all that good. We've been trailing a kidnapped scientist for a week and be have traced him to a ship that left the harbor about an hour and a half ago."

"What's the name of the ship?" the pilot asked.

"The *Kyushu Maru*."

"No sweat, Lieutenant, we can catch up with the ship."

"But there's a problem, a bomb is set to go off on the ship in less than an hour."

The pilot lifted off the vacant lot and headed south over Lower Manhattan and out to sea. They flew down the coastline for several miles as the pilot buzzed various ships trying to locate the *Kyushu Maru*.

"That bad boy has got to be down there somewhere," the pilot said as they continued along the coastline.

About fifteen minutes later they spotted the ship. Detective Sinclair keyed the loudspeaker. "Ahoy, the *Kyushu Maru*, this is the New York Police Department. Ask permission to come aboard."

Captain Takeda was on the bridge and he signaled

his approval.

The three detectives strapped on canvas belts and the pilot lowered them down to the deck of the ship.

"Captain, I'm Lieutenant Scott Dula of the New Orleans Police Department. We believe you have two stowaways on board."

"No, Lieutenant, so sorry, only our crew on board."

"My guess is that they are hidden in a crate from the House of Fong Imports and Exports bound for Shanghai."

"Yes, we have such a crate on board, but there is nothing unusual about the shipment."

"Captain, could you get your men to open the container and bring out the crate?"

"Of course."

Dula knew he had to tell the Captain about the bomb in plenty of time for him and his crew to man the lifeboats and that time was running out for it was already ten minutes after six.

The crew opened the container and pulled out the crate from the House of Fong.

"Now, open it up," Dula said.

The men used crowbars to open the wooden crate. They removed all of the contents but found no stowaways.

Dula was disappointed.

"Okay, Captain, we've caused you a lot of trouble for nothing and we apologize for that."

"That's all right, Lieutenant, as you boys say, no sweat."

The Captain issued the orders to close the crate but Dula heard a noise that sounded like someone kicking. He crawled inside the crate as the kicking sound became louder.

"Captain, I believe we have something. Give me a crowbar."

He frantically pried the boards off the false bottom of the crate and saw Macee wiggling and kicking. "Ms. Marineaux, I presume."

Dula knew they had only minutes before the bomb was to explode. "Captain, I have some really bad news for you."

"Oh, what could it be?"

"There is a bomb on your ship and it is timed to explode in about twelve minutes, so I suggest you man your lifeboats and get off this ship right now!"

The Captain had a worried look on his face and seemed stunned for a minute. Then he barked the order to lower the lifeboats and abandon ship.

Francis and Sinclair strapped the canvas harness around V. J. and Macee, both still groggy, and the pilot lifted them off the deck of the ship and into the chopper, then sent the cables back down for the detectives.

Dula tapped the pilot on the shoulder. "Russ, can we hang around for a minute? I'd sure like to see that little Captain and his crew make it to safety."

"Sure, a few minutes."

The Captain and the crew of the ship worked feverishly dropping the lifeboats into the water and scrambled down rope ladders.

Dula began to sweat as he waited for the boats to clear the ship.

At exactly six thirty the bomb exploded and the force from the explosion shook the helicopter and sent high waves toward the lifeboats nearly capsizing them. Within five minutes the ship disappeared under the coastal waters.

"Whew, that was a close call," the pilot said. "I'll

alert the Coast Guard and tell them to pick up the Captain and his crew."

"Yeah, and I want to thank you boys for your help," Dula said.

"It was a pleasure working with you," Detective Sinclair said.

"Yeah, but you guys must live charmed lives," Hodges added.

They all laughed.

Macee rubbed her eyes and looked over at V. J. who was still under the influence of the sedative. She slapped him a couple of times, shook him and he began to stir.

"V. J., wake up, we're safe, we've been rescued."

"Wha – where are we?"

"On our way back to New York City and you remember Lieutenant Dula we saw on TV? This is him right here."

V. J. yawned and shook hands with Dula.

"You're hard to keep up with, Doctor. We've been tracking you for a week and I'm not sure your problems are over yet."

"What do you mean?"

"There will always be someone looking for you trying to steal that secret of yours, whatever it is. And some of those people are in New York City."

"Lieutenant, where we heading?" Hodges asked. "Back to the police station?"

"No I don't think so, take us to the piers, I've got an idea. By the way, where do the tramp steamers dock?"

"Some trampers come into Pier 44."

"Okay, we'll get off there."

Hodges set the helicopter down near Pier 44. Dula and Francis helped V. J. and Macee out of the aircraft.

"Watch your heads!" V. J. yelled over the roar of the rotor blades.

"You gonna' be okay, Lieutenant?" Sinclair asked.

"Yeah, and we couldn't have done it without you boys. And if you get down to New Orleans, look us up and we'll take you out on the town."

"We'll hold you to that someday," Hodges said. Then he revved the engine and lifted off the pier.

Dula dialed O'Leary and asked him to bring the two brief cases and footlocker to Pier 44. He and his friends arrived thirty minutes later.

Chapter Twenty-Seven

Lieutenant Dula walked out to the end of the pier and watched the giant ships unloading cargo from ports throughout the world. *What am I going to do with this guy and the girl and the all that money? I took an oath to uphold the law and the law is clear: I should turn it over to the proper authorities. But maybe there's another way.*

He opened one of the briefcases and took out a thousand dollars.

"What you doin'?" Francis asked.

"I've got an idea so you stay here with our friends and I'll be back soon."

"Should we go with you, Lieutenant?" V. J. asked.

"No, Charlie will take good care of you."

Dula walked along the pier for about a half-mile when he spotted a tramp steamer and saw the name *Sydney Star* painted on the side. He hurried up the gangplank where a boatswain's mate stopped him. "Can I help you?"

"Yes, I'm Lieutenant Scott Dula of the New Orleans Police Department in New York on special assignment. What is your captain's name?"

"Captain O'Keefe."

"I would like to speak with him."

"Follow me."

The boatswain's mate escorted him down a stairway into the galley where several of the seamen were eating and on to the officers' quarters. He rapped on the Captain's door. "Captain, there's someone to see you, says he's from New Orleans."

He opened the door.

"This is Lieutenant Dula."

"Miles O'Keefe here, the skipper of the *Star*. To what do I owe the honor of this visit, Lieutenant?"

"Captain, can we speak in private?"

"Yes, of course," he said, then asked the boatswain's mate to return to his post.

Dula studied the old Captain's wrinkled, weather-beaten face and guessed he had been at sea most of his life.

"Now, Lieutenant, what can I do for you?"

"Captain O'Keefe, where are you bound for?"

"We're a tramper and we stop at dozens of ports and unload cargo, then go on to other ports and pick up cargo and, during a period of time, we will make our way around the world."

"I presume you are based in Australia."

"Yes, in Sydney, as the name of our ship would imply."

"Are you bound for Australia?"

"Yes, but it may be months before we arrive back at our home port."

"Then, do you ever go into the islands?"

"Yes, of course, Fiji is one of our delivery points."

The Captain looks like the kind of man who will deal so I guess I'll make my move. Dr. Casstevens and his friend sure don't have anything to lose.

"I would like to purchase transport for two of my friends to Australia and on to Fiji. Do you have extra berths available?"

"Yes, but I question if this is the form of transportation your friends would desire. A vacation cruise would be much more desirable."

"They require very little, except privacy, particularly when you visit the various port cities."

"Then, perhaps I can help you."

"How much will you charge?"

"That will be two thousand each to Sydney, and another thousand on to Fiji. But remember, they may not arrive at their destination for eight or nine months."

"That's absolutely no problem for they need a lot of rest."

"Alright, I will welcome them aboard."

"Six thousand dollars, is that correct?"

"Yes, Lieutenant."

Dula carefully counted ten one-hundred-dollar bills and handed them to the Captain. "Here is a thousand and I'll pay the remainder when they board. By the way, when do you sail?"

"At midnight, four hours from now."

Dula extended his hand. "That's good. I'll have my friends here before midnight."

"Thank you, Lieutenant."

The Captain escorted Dula back up to the main deck and stood at the gangplank as he left the ship.

V. J. breathed a sigh of relief when he saw the Lieutenant walking back down the pier toward where they were waiting.

Dula didn't know exactly how to approach the subject of their boarding the tramp steamer and traveling to some remote destination. But he knew they would never be safe in their own homeland. *And isn't that a kick in the butt.*

"Dr. Casstevens, Ms. Marineaux, you have been through hell these past couple of weeks and you both must be very strong to have survived," Dula said.

"There have been sinister plots to try to kidnap you and, I guess, to learn what you know about certain scientific matters of which I have no knowledge. Now we must make some very important decisions."

"Lieutenant, Macee and I will always be in your debt for rescuing us," V. J. said. "And I don't know exactly what you are driving at, but we trust you and Detective Francis."

"Well, here's the deal – I've booked passage on a tramp steamer for you and your lady to Australia and on to the Fiji Islands. Perhaps the two of you can just disappear."

"Maybe, but we're broke, Lieutenant, and we need clothes and one other thing, Macee has a daughter whose name is Victoria who lives down in Golden Meadow in Louisiana with her grandmother. When we get settled we want her to come to live with us."

"I've got the money and clothes covered; the daughter, I'll have to work on that. Now Charlie, I want you to take Ms. Marineaux shopping and buy her everything she will need for a long journey and buy the Doctor whatever you think he will need and be back here by eleven o'clock."

Dula opened the briefcase again and pulled out two thousand dollars. "This ought to cover the clothes." Then he opened one of the briefcases and held it up to the light for V. J. to see.

V. J. had never seen that much money in his life. "Whew, where did you find it?"

"Fong had it, I think he ripped off the mob."

"Could I borrow a couple of grand?"

Dula removed the money from the briefcase and handed it to him.

Francis walked over to a pay phone booth and

called a taxi to Pier 44. V. J. joined him and whispered something in his ear and handed him the two thousand dollars. When the taxi arrived, the driver opened the back door for Macee and the detective then sped away.

V. J. was curious about the money. "Now, Lieutenant, tell me more about the money."

"You probably don't need to know but I believe it was part of the payoff money to be turned over to someone in New York in exchange for finding you. I think the chink was going to keep it."

"How much is in there?"

"A lot."

"Really, how much?"

"Looks like, maybe twenty-million."

"Whew! And you're going to give us some of it?"

"I'm going to give you all of it."

"Man, that's heavy!"

"Maybe this is destiny paying you back for what you've been through these past couple of weeks."

"Thanks, Lieutenant, now tell me what about Macee's daughter?"

"I'll take care of her. You can correspond with me under a pseudonym, something like 'Shaky' for I will always remember how groggy you were when we pulled you out of that crate on the freighter. When I know you are settled I'll make arrangements for her to join you, wherever you are."

Dula knew he would have to make up a tall tale to explain the doctor's disappearance and decided he would tell the people back in New Orleans that he and Ms. Marineaux perished on the *Kyushu Maru*.

Francis and Macee returned two hours later and unloaded several shopping bags from the taxi. The detective also handed a small package to V. J. who put it in his pocket.

Dula took four thousand dollars out of a briefcase for future travel expenses for Macee's daughter and then handed both of the briefcases to V. J.

"Okay, it's time," Dula said.

He and Francis -- carrying the footlocker -- escorted them to the *Sydney Star* to meet Captain O'Keefe.

The Captain was standing on the pier. "Welcome back, Lieutenant Dula, and these are your friends?"

"Yes, this is V. J. Casstevens and Macee Marineaux and they are very interested in world travel."

Dula handed him the additional five thousand dollars for the fare. "I know they will enjoy the dozens of ports 'o call on the itinerary of your ship. Please take good care of them. And would you ask your men to help with their luggage?"

The Captain returned to the ship.

Dula turned to V. J. "Okay, Doctor, you and Ms. Marineaux are good to go?"

Macee realized it was time to say goodbye to the detectives and began to cry. She hugged each of them and kissed them on the cheek.

V. J. extended his hand. "You know, Lieutenant, I had just about given up on trusting people until you and Charlie came along."

"Just doing our job, Doctor."

"No, it was a lot more than that. It was action born out of the character that both of you men possess and I'm darned proud to have been a part of your lives, even if it was only for a short time."

"I hope you have a safe voyage and find what you're looking for."

"Thank you, Lieutenant."

V. J. took Macee by the hand and walked up the

gangplank but stopped after only a few steps. "You know what, Macee, I've never been happier in my life. Seems like I've finally made peace with myself."

"That's good, V. J., real good."

"*Que vous etes belle.*"

"Oh, do you really mean it when you say I'm pretty? No one ever told me that before."

"Yes and I'm glad you're here with me and I want you to always be with me."

"I always will."

"*Je vous aim.*"

"I've waited two years to hear you say you love me," she said with a smile on her face and heaven in her eyes.

"Macee, how would you like for us to get married? Captain O'Keefe can do the ceremony."

"Oh, V. J., are you serious?" she asked, squeezing his hand. "You know there have been times when I didn't even think you liked me."

"Yeah, I know, but it wasn't you, Macee, I just didn't like myself and I'm sorry I wasn't nice to you. Will you marry me?"

"Yes, *je vous aime,* I've always loved you and more now than ever before. You are my *compagnon de voyage* forever."

V. J. reached down into his pocket and took out the small package.

"Here, I have something for you." He removed the wrapping.

Macee opened the small box and saw the beautiful diamond ring. "*Mon amour,* this is so special."

"Yeah, it's special for me, too."

He hugged her and led her up the gangplank to the main deck where the Captain was waiting for them.

The detectives watched from the pier as the ship moved out to sea.

Francis looked over at Dula and saw him wipe several tears away from his face.

"Scott, how much money was in the briefcase?"

"Twenty million."

Francis' breath caught in his throat and he couldn't speak for a couple of minutes.

"Twenty million, yeah, that's beautiful. Guess we're off the honor system."

"Guess so."

"Scott, you're the greatest."

"Yeah, I guess I am pretty good."

Both men walked away from the pier laughing.

The next morning Bruiser Brown found Alexander Culverwell unconscious in his wheel chair and rushed him to the hospital where the doctors informed him that one of the old man's lungs had collapsed. He died a few hours later.

That day all three television networks reported that Surgeon General Harrison Chamberlain had been arrested and charged with public corruption.

Luka Avanzini put out a five-million dollar contract on Wu-tang Fong but later learned he was in the custody of federal agents.

CHAPTER TWENTY-EIGHT

Ten years later *Sports World Magazine* carried an in-depth report on the Summer Olympics scheduled to begin the next week in Moscow.

The article focused on a woman from the Fiji Islands who was the favorite to win the one- and two-hundred-meter races and several other track events including the hurdles.

"She is a six-foot, one-hundred-forty pound runner by the name of Stephanie Steenburgen of the Fiji Islands, wife of wealthy Fijian planter, Colonel John Steenburgen," the article reported. "But there is something very unusual about Ms. Steenburgen. Believe it or not, she's a forty-year-old mother of four and already holds records in the Asia and Pan-American games. She's an odds-on favorite to capture as many as five gold medals in Moscow thus making her one of the most celebrated athletes in the history of the games."

The *World* also reported that her twenty-year-old daughter Victoria was favored to win the women's five- and ten-thousand-meter runs.

Two native Fijian runners will join Steenburgen and her daughter in the relay competition, the magazine noted.

"Several well-known physical fitness experts will be on hand in Moscow to interview Ms. Steenburgen and try to discover the source of her amazing athletic abilities – particularly at her age," the article said. "And scientists from various disciplines plan to visit Fiji to determine the influence the climate and food in the islands may have on the physical development of athletes like Ms. Steenburgen.

"Doctor Walker Bannister, the director of the Culverwell Institute in Chicago, named for the late philanthropist Alexander Culverwell, will lead the scientific expedition to the islands."

The article pointed out that anthropologists believe the life expectancy of the people in the Fiji and surrounding islands has increased dramatically during the past ten years. Their studies show that only a limited number of Fijians and the natives from all the surrounding islands die from anything other than old age and accidental death.

A man wearing sunglasses and a Panama hat climbed the steps to his reserved seat in the Moscow Olympic Stadium and waited eagerly for the women's one-hundred-meter race to begin.

The morning *Moscow Times* predicted that Steenburgen would win the event and could possibly set a new world record. However, the newspaper said she would face stiff competition from Andrea Walters of the United States and Nicole Marceau of France, both in their early twenties.

When the gun sounded, the man wearing the sunglasses and Panama hat stood and watched the race through a pair of binoculars.

Steenburgen had a fast start out of the blocks and soon took a commanding lead over the other runners in the event. When she crossed the finish line the crowd went wild, yelling and screaming, as the time clock showed she had set a new world record.

"That's my girl, Macee!" the man wearing the sunglasses and Panama hat shouted.

Then he made his way down out of the stands to the dressing rooms where Macee was waiting for him. "Hey beautiful, that was spectacular. You're wonderful and I'm so proud of you."

She threw her arms around him and kissed him. "Pretty good, eh?"

After the games ended they returned to the Islands to the sugar plantation where V. J. had set up a state-of-the-art laboratory for his continuing research into aging.

One day as he was eating breakfast on the patio of their mansion near the seashore, he opened the mail and saw a clipping from the New Orleans newspaper about the retirement of Captain Scott Dula from the police force after thirty-five years of service. The article pointed out that Dula had received nationwide recognition for solving the Research Center murders in the city ten years earlier.

"Of the thirteen men involved in the killings, five died in a shootout with mobsters in Chicago, seven are in the federal penitentiary and, Alexander Culverwell, the man reported to be the mastermind behind the killings, died before being indicted by a grand jury," the article said.

V. J. picked up the phone and dialed New Orleans.

"Yeah, this is Dula."

"Captain, eh?"

"How you doing, Shaky?"

"Not too bad. Hear about Macee?"

"Saw it on TV last week. I'm proud of her, both of you."

"So you retired."

"Yeah, got a gold watch and a thank-you from the

grateful people of New Orleans. And they retired my
shield in the Police Academy Museum, guess that's
something."

"Yes, it's a wonderful tribute."

"I'm bored stiff and I lost my old friend Charlie
Francis last week, couple of punks shot him when he
went to investigate an alarm at a convenience store. He
had just made sergeant."

"Charlie was a wonderful man and I know you miss
him."

"He was my best friend."

"Everything else okay, I mean you been feeling
good?"

"My wavy black hair has waved goodbye, but other
than that, yeah, I feel pretty good."

"As Macee would say *cela est la vie* – that's life. Now,
I've got an idea. Why don't you fly out here and let's renew some of your youth and vigor?"

"I guess that stuff really does work, take Macee and
all."

"Yeah, it works, why don't you come see us?"

"Well, maybe, but I'm a little short on cash."

"Man, no problem, I've got plenty, thanks to you –
and the Chinese," V. J. said as they both laughed. "I'll
send you a ticket first thing tomorrow."

"Okay, Shaky, why not? You've always been about
half crazy and maybe I'll just go crazy with you."

Macee walked up behind V. J and put her hands
over his eyes. "Peek-a-boo, guess who?"

V. J. turned in his chair, grabbed her around the
waist and pulled her down onto his lap where he gave
her a sweet, good-morning kiss.

"You sure look pretty in the morning sun and I love
you."

"I love you, too, and guess what – you've made me the happiest woman in the world. When I count my blessings, I count you twice."

V. J. smiled and kissed her again.

"You are my *joie de vivre*, my joy of living. So, who was that on the phone?"

"Scott Dula, he made Captain and now he's retired. And Charlie Francis was killed last week."

"Oh no, I've always had a very special place in my heart for Charlie. We owe him and Scott so much."

"There's also some good news. Scott is coming to see us. Thought I would give him a couple of treatments. I wish Charlie was coming with him."

"That would be wonderful."

He took her by the hand and they walked down to a blue lagoon under the cocoanut and pandanus trees where they could hear the waves breaking fifty yards out just beyond the yellow and pink coral reef.

"You know, Macee, I want to spend the rest of my life here on the islands with you and helping these islanders realize their dreams," he said as he held her in his arms beside the beautiful blue waters.

"I'll always be here for you, *mon amour*," she replied as she hugged and kissed him and wiped the tears from his eyes.

Bill Keith is an award-winning journalist who served as an investigative reporter, city editor and editor of three newspapers in Louisiana and Texas. He was a war correspondent in Vietnam and also had assignments in Tokyo, the Philippines and West Berlin and traveled in 35 other countries.

He earned the bachelor of arts degree in writing/journalism from Wheaton College in Illinois, the master of divinity from the Southwestern Baptist Theological Seminary in Fort Worth, Texas, and received a graduate diploma from the Tokyo School of the Japanese Language.

Through the years he served as the director of public relations for the Baptist General Convention of Texas; a Louisiana state senator representing the people of Shreveport; senior editor of Huntington House Books, Inc.; and president and chief fundraiser for the Academic Freedom Legal Defense Fund.

Keith has written 20 books -- both fiction and non-fiction -- including *Days of Anguish, Days of Hope* (Doubleday); *The Commissioner* (Pelican Publishing Co.); *Scopes II/the Great Debate* and *The Divine Connection* (Huntington House, Inc.); *Joy Comes in the Morning* (MV Press); *W. A. Criswell/the Authorized Biography* (Fleming Revell); *Gettin' Old Ain't for Sissies* (Stonegate Book Publishing Co., Inc.); *The Prayer Bag and Other Stories that Warm the Heart* (Stonegate Book Publishing Co., Inc.); and others. Several of the books are available on the internet through the author's website at www.BillKeithBooks.com.

He and his wife Vivian Marie live in Longview, Texas, where he works as a full time writer. His email address is Stonegatebooks@aol.com.

Other Books by Bill Keith

The Commissioner is the intriguing true story of death and deception and reveals a corrupt political battle during the 1970s that threatened Shreveport, Louisiana. The city's police commissioner -- the most powerful lawman in the state -- was behind multiple scandals including racism, payoffs, theft of city funds and tampering with a grand jury. He may also have been involved in the murder of an advertising executive who was scheduled to testify against him in court. (*Available at your local book store*)

Days of Anguish, Days of Hope is the story of Chaplain Robert Preston Taylor who spent 42 months in Japanese prison camps during World War II. When the Japanese bombed Pearl Harbor on Dec. 7, 1941, and Manila, the Philippines, the next day, Taylor was caught in a maelstrom of war. He ministered to the fighting men on the front lines during the Battle for Bataan and, after a daring rescue mission of several wounded American soldiers, received the Silver Star for bravery. He endured the Bataan Death March – where thousands of American soldiers died – the Cabanatuan Prison Camp, and the so-called "hell ships" that were bombed by American pilots who did not know the American prisoners were on board. He later was transferred to Japan, then Korea and finally Manchuria where he was liberated. He returned home to learn that his wife Ione, who was told he had died on the "hell ships," had remarried. However, he decided to continue his ministry to American soldiers and in 1962 President John F. Kennedy appointed him Air Force Chief of Chaplains with the rank of Major General.

Joy Comes in the Morning is the true story of one of the greatest miracles of the Twentieth Century. Delores Winder, a Presbyterian lady, was an invalid for 19 years and was planning her funeral when God intervened in her life. She was completely healed during a United Methodist Church Conference on the Holy Spirit in Dallas, Texas, in 1975. Since that time she and her husband Bill have traveled throughout the world telling her amazing story. (Available at www.BillKeithBooks.com)

Gettin' Old Ain't for Sissies is a motivational/inspirational book to help the baby boomers and older survive and enjoy the senior years. The thesis is: "Old age doesn't have to be the end of the line. It can be a bright new beginning." The book outlines the five things a person must do to live a vigorous lifestyle into the 70s, 80s and even the 90s and gives numerous examples of Older Champions.

The Prayer Bag and Other Stories that Warm the Heart tells the story of a missionary in Sumatra who prayed for a nail and found one in a can of Mandarin Oranges; a Christian who shared his faith with Emperor Hirohito of Japan after World War II; a holocaust survivor who forgave a concentration camp guard who had brutalized her sister who died in the camp; and a state senator who prayed through a difficult situation and won a great victory. It also tells the story of the author's wife who carries a prayer bag with her everywhere she goes. *(Available on www.BillKeithBooks.com)*

Look for these books in the future: *The Guns of Winter* (A novel about one man's war with Washington); *W. A. Criswell/the Authorized Biography* about the dynamic pastor of the First Baptist Church of Dallas, Texas, and a man believed by some to be the greatest preacher of the Twentieth Century; *Days of Rage* about the Tulsa, Oklahoma, race riot of 1921 where white vigilantes killed some 300 black people and destroyed 1200 homes; *Whisper in the Wind*, a novel about love and war in the South Pacific during World War II; *The Rise and Fall of Practically Everything* about the culture war that is raging all across America; *Scopes II/the Great Debate*, the story of the creation/evolution war in America; *The Incredible Journey*, the life story of Frank Bower who was in the *Mafia* for 19 years and served as the personal bodyguard to *Mafia don* John Gotti but today ministers to the homeless, runaway children, teenage prostitutes, alcoholics and addicts; *Escape to Lo Debar*, a biblical novel about a crippled boy by the name of Mephibosheth, son of Jonathan the son of King Saul and friend of King David; *The Shantung Revival* about one of the greatest revivals in history; and *Epiphanies and Other Divine Encounters* about people who have seen angels and had other divine experiences.